BELLY

OF

SALT

T.S. CHALK

Belly of Salt

Copyright ©2024 by T.S. Chalk.

All rights reserved.

No part of this publication may be reproduced, distributed, or transmitted in any form or by any means, including photocopying, recording, or other electronic or mechanical methods, without the prior written permission of the publisher, except as permitted by U.S. copyright law.

The story, all names, characters, and incidents portrayed in this production are fictitious. No identification with actual persons (living or deceased), places, buildings, and products is intended or should be inferred.

Published in the United States of America by:

Heron House Press LLC
Richmond, VA

1st Edition: September 2024

ISBN-13: 979-8-9912565-1-3

HERON HOUSE
- PRESS -

To Giggy.

8 months after

EVA CHOKED as the wind punched a gulp of icy air into her throat. Dagger-sharp gusts squeezed tears from the creases of her eyelids, stinging them blind. The wetness turned to ice on her cheeks, freezing long before it could leak from her jaw and dissipate into the wind.

She felt the wind clawing at her ears, but could not hear it. Instead, she heard ringing – a steady, pealing note with no obvious source. She remembered heat, and a hard shock of pressure like a punch from an enormous fist, pummeling her entire body. She remembered being afraid.

The ringing faded, and the huge noise of the wind finally boomed in her head. It deafened her, drowning every sound except its own thunderous rush over her ears. It dawned on Eva that she could not see because her eyes would not open – they were stuck shut, frozen by the wind and the tears it had extracted. She brought her hands to her face and they came in jerks, batted by the gale. She pressed icy fingers to her eyes and rubbed.

Eva saw trees. Through her tears, the cold, and the wind, she saw trees like a thick green carpet, smothering the ground far below.

She could not feel the floor beneath her feet. She twisted, putting her back to the treetops, and saw the *Thread Cutter* in flight, a dark and graceful corvette – swing-wing, atmo-capable. She saw ugly wounds in its hull and a wan ribbon of smoke trailing behind.

She was falling, and she screamed as she realized. She could scarcely hear the sound over the wind, though it came from her own mouth. Others were falling, too, and they all wore matching, black-speckled camouflage uniforms. They were nearby, some mere feet from her, in freefall racing her to the treetops. By ones and twos, their descent was halted with jarring decisiveness, plucked out of the race as their parachutes deployed. Eva twisted to face the treetops and her fingers scrabbled at her shoulder, searching for the parachute ripcord, finding only the soft cloth of her jacket.

More tears froze in the wind. She was not wearing her parachute.

Another soldier in a black uniform fell nearby, and Eva reached out to him with hands that had lost sensation in the icy gale. The soldier saw, and reached for her in turn. They both shouted – pleas, commands, prayers, all of it meaningless, drowned in the roar of the wind as they drifted toward one another, angling bodies to control their flight. They met, but not with the gentle touch of fingertips that the slowness of their progress implied. They collided with a grunting glut of arrested momentum as the wind, undeterred by her plight, continued to shriek in her ears. The soldier brought his mouth to her ear, and although his words were simple, he screamed them just to be heard.

"Ten seconds!"

Eva wrapped her legs around his waist and laced her arms through the straps and webbing of his gear. Belts and pouches all became loops and grips for her fingers and limbs. She found every fold of fabric that could offer even a scrap of traction, and squeezed so tightly that her muscles shook as she braced for the pain.

The soldier yanked on his ripcord, and the parachute deployed. Eva's fingernails bent and then snapped in a fraction of a second, some ripping cleanly off, overwhelmed by the enormity of the deceleration. Her arm was laced through the straps of his gear, and she felt, rather than heard, a wet popping like a bubble in thick syrup, as the joint of one shoulder was torn from its fitted socket. Her arms slithered out from his gear and straps. She slid down him, her lips losing their skin on his clothing, and her teeth clacking off his buckles.

She fell, and he did not.

She spun as she plummeted now. The treetops were closer, and her dislocated arm flapped in the wind, spouting pain. The wind was just as sharp but it no longer froze her lungs to breathe – nearer to the ground, the air was warmer. As she rotated, she saw that she was still not alone – an unlucky handful of other black-uniformed soldiers kept pace with her fall. Some still clawed at their shoulders, unable to accept that the ripcord was not there, mouths open with cries Eva could not hear. Others were running, legs pumping cartoonishly in mid-air as feral instinct screamed at them to escape. A final few fell calm and lifeless, their limbs fluttering limply in the wind. Eva tasted vomit.

The wind buffeted her, turned her, and she spotted the *Thread Cutter* far away and falling fast. The thin streamer of smoke had become a billowing river of black, rushing from the ship's distant silhouette. The craft was listing hard, almost fully sideways, nose inclined towards the ground.

Again a gust twisted her, and she saw a new, odd form falling nearby. It was big and mechanical, massively humanoid with steel arms, legs, and a torso. Even through her terror and the icy wind, Eva was startled. It was a freight lift, a heavy steel ground vehicle used to move cargo containers, painted lemon-yellow and in freefall alongside her. It belonged even less than she did, plummeting through empty sky.

She would dig her own grave when she hit, smashing a patch of dirt into pulpy mud alongside the handful of other parachute-less soldiers who matched her fall nearby. Not the lucky soldiers above her, of course, now floating to safety on parachute silk – some in the sky had come prepared.

Eva tucked her body into a slim javelin and sliced through the air toward the falling freight lift. The treetops were close, and the lemon-yellow machine was the only wildcard left – the only thing in all the wide, cold sky that might, somehow, have a parachute.

HE WAS tall for his age, or had been a few years ago. As he walked, he leaned a bit toward the bicycle at his side, a slight hunch in his shoulders down toward the handlebars, as though he might jump on and pedal at any moment. His bicycle's paint flaked in a few spots and was sun-bleached throughout, once a bold blue, but now a wan aquamarine. Nonetheless, the chain glinted with oil and the teeth on the gears were sharp.

The young man's boots were well-worn under their layer of dust, cracks spiderwebbing across the pinched folds wherever the leather bunched as he stepped, but the signs of wear did not exceed the curiously comfortable deterioration unique to thick cowhide.

Ample stitching crawled along the outskirts of each leathery flap, a time-consuming and old-fashioned approach to construction when new shoes could be made in minutes on a home printer, in any style or color available in thousands of fab files on the feed. Where simpler, printed shoes might have frayed or collapsed, however, his boots absorbed the stresses of hard use and exhibited that abuse by curving and softening, fitting the young man's toes quite comfortably.

In short, his boots were well-built, long-lasting, and at one point, expensive. This put them at odds with the rest of him – his bicycle, his clothing, his haircut, and possibly even the young man himself all had an air of bare serviceability. They did the job, for cheap, and did not pretend anything more.

He walked his bicycle to a halt in front of an angular orange lift of smallish stature, only tall enough to need a short steel step for access to the cockpit. The lift was crouched in a parking stance, canopy resting over its haunches and manipulators wrapped neatly in front. Every machine for sale on the lot was a bipedal lift, colossally humanoid in their pattern with two legs, a torso-like canopy housing the cockpit, and magnetic cargo forks integrated into the arms. The engine embedded in this lift's back was painted with snappy colors – orange on the main housing cover to match the exterior paint, yellow on the spray of exhaust pipes that arched from its back, and even the rubber hoses had a faint black gleam.

A plastic sign on the lift read:

```
BOWEN-HITACHI
FREIGHT STALLION
13 HOURS
$222,000
OWNER-OPERATOR FINANCING AVAILABLE
RENT-TO-BUY!
```

The young man moved on.

The lot was large and deep and the only source for used lifts within a manageable distance for someone who usually got places on a bicycle.

It was organized by price with the most expensive lifts at the front, surrounded by crisp signs and smooth pavement. The back of the lot had a sort of grim pragmatism – dusty lifts and unkempt grass, with hints of a junkyard at the farthest end. The young man stopped in front of another lift, this one painted dark blue and much larger than the first, with a ladder to assist the climb to the cockpit. Its plastic sign read:

```
HERSHAW MFG
MDL 70-D
156 HOURS
$161,500
```

The young man hopped on his bicycle and pedaled towards the back of the lot. His skin was smooth and unblemished under a layer of road dust, and his fingernails were squarely cut, recently. He relaxed his grip on the handlebars as he worked the pedals, enjoying the warm emptiness of the lot. His tires were new, purchased for this trip, and he liked watching dirt roll under the fresh black treads.

He pedaled on, skipping past a dozen lifts without checking their costs. With the tidy front of the lot well behind him, he saw tufts of grass growing with reedy optimism underneath the well-used lifts now surrounding him.

He slowed to a stop in front of a lift with paint that was green under a hint of surface corrosion, and peered at its plastic sign.

```
HERSHAW MFG
MDL 38-A
1,372 HOURS
$41,700
```

His eyebrows drew together as he looked ahead, finding very little of the lot remaining before he reached the back, and the very cheapest lifts. He rode forward, his front wheel dipping into a puddle as he pushed hard on the pedals, tires slickening with mud, jostling over the harsh lip where the path gave way to the rut of the puddle.

He pedaled in silence to the very back of the lot and eyed the lifts around him worriedly. Many were sprawled in heaps, missing limbs or with engine bays gaping empty on their backs. Few had paint of any meaningful color and the grasses grew tall here, poking cheerful green leaflets through the drab mechanical appendages. The young man leaned his bicycle up against one of the rusted hulks and picked his way between the puddles and greenery, checking the plastic signs on the least-decrepit lifts.

```
ANSHIN TOOL CMPNY
TYPE 02
9,568 HOURS
$6,800

HERSHAW MFG
MDL 55-A
5,563 HOURS
$9,700

HERSHAW MFG
MDL 70-B
3,799 HOURS
$10,500
```

The young man sighed, and a gust of wind rattled the grass and signs around him. At length, he began walking the complete perimeter of the lot, checking the signs on each lift with methodical pragmatism. He hopped around puddles and clambered over rusting piles of steel appendages. Some lifts were stacked on top of one another in piles that listed under the weight of their irregularly shaped constituents, limbs entangled. He eyed them all with ever-increasing dismay.

The lot was roughly rectangular, and as the young man approached a far corner, he spotted a green-and-black lift crowded in with several other derelict machines. The young man peered around the limbs and bodies of the lifts blocking his view, keeping his face flat and expressionless as though the bargain he searched for might spook at the sight of his hopefulness.

The green-and-black lift looked to be in good order. It had all four of its limbs and simple, forked manipulators that looked suitable for box-shaped cargo. A large, stout-looking engine rode its back, and four exhaust pipes emerged from the top of the motor with uniform straightness. The paint was dusty but the colors underneath were strong.

The young man checked its plastic sign fearfully.

```
HERSHAW MFG
MDL 49-???
??? HOURS
$4950
```

In his back pocket, compressed in the warm leather of his wallet and slightly damp with sweat, five paper bills waited to be spent. Each bill was marked for $1000, and four of the five bills had flexed and flopped when the young man slipped them into the wallet hours before. Only one was still crisp, not frayed and supple after many months of being taken in and out of the wallet to be stared at and pensively rolled between his fingers.

The young man climbed the short ladder to the cockpit and examined what he could of the engine – the blocky steel and arcing rubber tubing revealed no obvious leaks, holes or missing components. He grabbed the handle to the cockpit's side door, pulled, and the door opened with a pained squeak. The young man climbed into the cockpit and swung himself down into the driver's seat.

The cockpit was dusty but the windshield was largely free of grime. The young man surveyed the rusting, grassy lot from the view of a lift operator with some excitement – he had watched hours of instructional videos, but had never sat in the cockpit of a lift before today.

The seat had pleasant give under his rear. There were four pedals in a row by his feet, two equipped with straps and buckles that dangled unused, and two more bare metal pedals in the middle. At chest height, large control sticks poked out like an insect's antenna from the control panel, each encrusted with buttons for his fingers. He grabbed them and twisted, exercising the sticks through their full range of motion. They clicked back and forth, eliciting no response from the lift.

The young man released the sticks and wiped his hand over the dashboard, clearing a swathe in the canvas of dust that covered the instrumentation. He rummaged through the storage bins on his right and left, finding only grit and discarded wrappers, then tapped a button on the cockpit's ceiling. A small compartment obediently flapped open, dropping something into his lap.

The object was small and plastic, emblazoned with the stylized horse logo of the Hershaw Manufacturing Company. The young man's heart leapt as he realized it was the ignition badge, then sank when he realized the presence of that critical piece meant the lift must be immobile – no lift dealer would leave the ignition badge inside a functional lift. The young man sighed and tossed the ignition badge on the dashboard.

He found a button on the dashboard labeled ACC POWER and pushed it hopefully. To his surprise, the lift responded.

The engine mounted behind the firewall at his back remained lifeless, but the young man heard a faint mechanical whirring and the lights on the dashboard illuminated all at once, needle-style analog gauges sweeping their full range of motion. After a few seconds, the gauges rested and the lights went out save for a small green indicator on the far side of the control panel. The young man wiped the dust away from the console around the lit green bulb.

START CHECK

The cheerful green bulb squatted just to the right of the text, and was now the only light on the entirety of the panel. Hope welled in the young man's breast despite his efforts to remain skeptical.

Above his head, he found a round red dial switch labeled ENGINE MAIN. He grabbed the switch and twisted it. Behind him, the engine gave a subdued moan, less than a second in duration, and then quieted. He twisted the round switch again, then once more. Each time the short, quiet noise from behind him, then silence.

The young man let out a long sigh and sat back in the chair. He poked indolently at a few buttons on the dashboard, causing the windshield wipers to scrape across the dry windshield. Another toggle sounded a horn outside, startling him upright in the seat with its blaring note. A third button lit a red light above the words AUX HEATER, the letters scrawled by hand in white, flaking paint. Throughout it all, the lift's engine remained inert.

"Engine's shot!" The shout came from outside.

The young man saw a figure standing outside, arms folded, watching him through the windshield, and he quickly abandoned his seat inside the cockpit for the narrow step outside the cab. A cool wind blew across his nose, wicking away sweat that had formed in the cockpit's warm confines.

"How much to get it running?" The young man shouted as he began descending the ladder.

He hopped down the last rung and landed with a puff of dust, turning to find a man with a crisp white shirt tucked into stained work pants behind him. The man was thin-boned and old enough to be a father twice over, and the contrast between his shabby pants and gleaming white shirt was jarring.

"More than I'm asking for it now. It's been a bit since I looked at it, but if I remember right, the engine is completely seized up. Total loss. I even tried to get it to turn over by hand – wouldn't budge. I'm Arnold."

Arnold extended his hand, and they shook.

"Iskander," the young man replied.

Arnold's thin hand was dusty, and his grip was firm.

"Nice to meet you. I own this lot, so if you want to buy one of these lifts, you'll have to come see me at the main office. Normally you'd see my wife while I run the tools, but she's out today. Makes you a little lucky – she might try to sell this hulk to you."

Arnold faced the green-and-black lift with an appraising eye.

"I'm remembering it better, now that we're standing here. The paint looks fresh, but the engine's never run a single time and that's only the start of its problems. The 49 is a good chassis but this one's got parts in it I've never seen. Bargain suppliers, most likely, not making their parts to OEM spec and then skipping out on warranty support."

Iskander turned to look at the green-and-black lift, somewhat wistfully.

"I guess that's why the price is what it is."

Arnold nodded, then gave Iskander a hard look.

"Ever drive a lift before?"

Iskander shook his head.

"Nope. But it seems like good work."

"It is. I got some good starter lifts on the lot, something you could take the pilot's exam in, get your feet wet in the yard."

Arnold took a personal out of his pocket and swiped his finger on it a few times, eyes intent on the screen.

"Mostly gas-powered, but a few electric. You won't be wanting those unless you're way down under the mitt, though. If you look on the widefeed, everyone will tell you electric, electric, electric, but not on Sargasso."

Above them, the sky glowed a constant, harsh white – Sargasso's peculiar atmosphere of startlingly hostile sunlight made livable by thick and constant cloud cover. The clouds created a pleasant climate complete with seasonal temperature swings, but clouds alone could not stop the energetic sun's constant, saturating bombardment of electromagnetic interference. Sargassi buildings were laced with electronic shielding that permitted most devices to operate normally indoors while buried cables established a surprisingly robust planet-wide feed – like anyone else, Sargassi could watch their favorite shows, see which friends' engagement photos had more ambition than budget, and attend interminable video conferences, but only as long as a solid roof stood overhead. Outside, signal bars dropped to zero and the unlucky could even get caught in one of Sargasso's periodic solar storms, which were harmless to flesh-and-blood but could fuse unshielded tech inoperable.

"Sooner or later you'll get caught in a squall and any e-motor will lock up on you," Arnold said. "Good ole' gas is the way to go. Where are you looking for work?"

"Picochee is my closest mitt."

Arnold looked up from his personal. "Picochee? Near South Hampton?"

Iskander nodded.

"And you got here on that?" Arnold gestured at Iskander's bicycle, leaning nearby against a heap of machinery.

Iskander nodded again, and Arnold blew out a loud breath.

"Lord above, you must really want a lift."

Iskander nodded a third time, and Arnold turned towards the front of the lot.

"Come on, I got some good models for you. Not too expensive, but they run right, you got my word."

Iskander didn't move, and his eyebrows were tight with concern.

"I've already looked over what you have up there, and it's too much."

"Normally I'd save this question for later in the negotiations, but if you don't mind – how much you got to spend?"

Iskander pointed at the green-and-black lift.

"That."

Arnold's personal pinged an alert, and he seemed to forget Iskander existed as he tapped out a response. Finally, he pocketed the device and looked at Iskander with his hands on his hips.

"Sorry to say, but that's not a lift. The lifts are up front. These …" Arnold gestured at the sad machines surrounding them, "… these are parts. Just junk."

He jerked his chin at the green-and-black lift.

"That only reason that's still in one piece is that I haven't needed a part out of it yet. Now, I'm sorry, I got someone waiting up front. Come up and see me if you decide on something."

Arnold spun on his heels as he spoke, the hems of his pants sweeping arcs in the dirt behind his shoes. A moment later, he was gone.

ISKANDER STOOD amid sighing wind and machinery. He looked at the green-and-black lift and puffed a wistful breath through his teeth. Even crouched in its parking stance, the lift was tall enough to tower above him.

The sun was strong now, high overhead, and the cracked rubber of his bicycle's handlebar was hot under his palm as he pulled the bicycle up by his side. He walked the bicycle all the way to the final unexplored corner of the lot, winding around the browned and decaying lifts and walking the soggy, sloping edges of puddles to avoid standing water. Periodically, he peered at plastic signs, and came away from each looking disheartened.

He doubled back, with faltering resolution, to sweep the lot one last time for miracles somehow missed during his search. Many minutes later, as the sun sent sweat trickling down his ribcage, he found his way back to the green-and-black lift.

An odd, glinting light was shining around its dusty windshield – the headlights that dotted each of the four corners shone with a hard yellow glow, turned on by his earlier, fumbling exploration of the dashboard. Iskander kicked out the stand on his bicycle and mounted the ladder to the cockpit.

For the second time that day, he expressed a small puff of dust from the cushion as the seat took his weight. The dashboard and the view from the cockpit gave him the same prickle of excitement as before, but now, the sensation only made him feel foolish. He sat for a few moments in the quiet shade of the cockpit, his face gloomy. The ignition badge still lay where he had left it on the dashboard, and he held it in his palm, staring at the logo, before placing it back into the overhead storage tray. He closed the tray cover slowly, feeling the shudder in the plastic as it clicked into place, and looked at the dashboard dejectedly.

"Fuck." The dusty cockpit absorbed the word as he said it.

He found the switch for the headlights and flipped it to the off position, then reset the remaining buttons and toggles to the best of his recollection.

When only the green START CHECK light remained, Iskander reached for the ACC POWER button, which would render the whole lift lifeless once again.

His hand hovered above the button, and after a few moments of hesitation he instead blew out a sigh and reached up to the round, red ENGINE MAIN dial switch to give it one final turn.

A guttural murmur reverberated through his spine – the back of the seat was flush against the steel firewall that separated the cockpit from the engine bay. The engine was issuing a low but animated rumble, and as Iskander kept pressure on the dial switch, the lift's entire cabin began to vibrate around him. A second later, the engine sputtered, caught, and then thundered to a husky, loping idle that rattled his teeth through the firewall.

He released the dial switch and sat rigidly in the seat. The engine's coughing reverberations calmed after a few seconds, becoming a gentle but constant push at his back. More seconds passed, and Iskander waited for the engine to stall. Half a minute had elapsed before he realized that the dashboard was now alive with colored indicators and oscillating needles housed within gauges, while the engine rumbled at a confident, steady idle behind him.

Iskander rested his hands on the lift's control sticks and pushed them upward. The cockpit's bulkheads groaned and outside, the lift's arm-like manipulators responded, tracking upward to match the control sticks' travel and sending small avalanches of dust billowing to the ground.

Iskander released the control sticks nervously and they snapped back to their center position, spring loaded, as the lift's manipulators came to a halt outside the cockpit.

A button above his head was labeled MAIN KILL. The engine loped at idle behind the firewall at his back, and Iskander considered the button solemnly for several moments. The lift had refused to start just twenty minutes ago, and with no determinable change in between, it now started with gusto. There was, however, only one way to determine if it would start again.

Iskander reached up and pushed MAIN KILL.

The engine behind him shuddered to silence, rocking the lift's frame as it came to a halt and lacing the cabin with the tangy scent of unburned fuel.

Iskander shifted his hand back to the ENGINE MAIN dial switch and held the air inside his lungs. His head bowed in something approaching prayer, he closed his eyes and turned the dial switch.

The engine snarled immediately to life, and a broad grin split Iskander's face in half.

The lift worked, at least sometimes. From what Iskander had seen on the lot that day, ₱4950 for a lift that worked, sometimes, was an earth-shattering bargain – one that would evaporate the moment Arnold learned that the lift's motor could turn over under its own power.

Iskander killed the engine once more, pocketed the ignition badge, and clambered out of the cockpit at a startling pace. He ignored the ladder and jumped straight to the ground, landing with a thud next to his bicycle.

He pedaled hard down the weedy path, his speed climbing as it smoothed near the well-kempt lifts up front, until he was racing on level pavement towards the only structure on the entirety of the lot – the buying office.

The building was a simple plasticrete dome with prefabricated doors and windows bolted to the smooth, matte grey exterior, covering holes cut in the shell after the plasticrete hardened. The dome ballooned out of the flat expanse of the lot, like a melon sliced in half and placed wet side down on a cutting board.

The sturdy and inexpensive structures fulfilled basic storage needs around industrial centers, but they could make cheap housing, too. Iskander found the smooth gray walls comforting and remembered that when many were clustered together, they looked like strips of the sweetened vitamins his minders had given him as a child, each pill housed in its own plastic bubble, until the pressure of a thumb burst them free.

A small parking area with two lonely-looking cars separated the maze of used lifts from the domed office. The cars were egglike publicly-owned models, metal on the bottom half with sloping glass on the top. The fares on public cars were reasonable, but still many times more expensive than pedaling his bicycle from place to place.

As he neared the domed office, Iskander coasted, letting momentum carry his wheels over the tiny lip where the paved surface of the lot met the dome's plasticrete base. There was no landscaping or decoration at all, although two short benches flanked the office's door to provide some humanity.

The interior was a cool, dim office space where the walls were lined with gray rubber, the remains of the balloon that gave the structure shape while the plasticrete was still wet. Arnold sat behind one of two desks in the room, head in his hands as he stared unhappily at a large touchscreen. The other desk was empty, and aside from a few chairs and a brochure stand that held some colorful leaflets, the rest of the spherical room was bare.

Arnold raised his head from his hands as Iskander entered.

"You're back." Arnold's voice was surprised but not pleased.
"Never left, actually." Iskander kept his voice cheerful.
"Find anything you liked?"
"Yep. The green-and-black Hershaw 49 with the shot engine."
Arnold regarded Iskander for several moments before he spoke.
"Why?"
"I think I can fix it up."
Arnold squinted at him. "You work on lifts?"
Iskander shook his head.
"Nope, but I like a challenge."
Arnold paused, then blew out a heavy breath.
"Okay," he said the word with bemused acceptance. "It's sold completely as-is, no guarantees and no refunds. Clear on that?"
Iskander nodded.
"You'll have three hours to get it off the lot. After that I charge rent, a hundred per day."
He opened a drawer in his desk and Iskander could hear papers being shuffled.
"You can pay someone to come in here and move it, *if* they show me a pilot's license. You may *not* borrow any equipment from me. But I can move it for you with one of my lifts for $300 flat. I'll also put it on a truck for you, but you have to hire the truck yourself. If you can't get a truck today, I'll put it by the road for pickup."
Arnold banged the drawer shut, empty-handed despite his paper shuffling, and muttered to himself. He stood and walked with hard, smacking footsteps over to another desk where he opened a different drawer, pulled a handful of paperwork, and leaned over the desk to begin writing on it.
"Remind me of the price?"
The price had been $4950 – Iskander remembered it clearly, as it was just $50 shy of everything he had.
"Forty-five hundred," Iskander said the number with conviction, then squinted his eyes in confused recollection. "And some change, maybe? Sorry, I can't remember."
"I'll just give it to you for forty-five."
Iskander nodded and thought it wise to not volunteer more conversation, so he turned and paced around the room, examining the limited distractions. A colorful leaflet for a lift repair shop was nestled on the brochure stand, and Iskander plucked it. The paper was cool to the

touch and printed with pictures of massive lifts and promises of honest service. Iskander folded the leaflet, the paper stiffening as it compressed, and slipped it into his back pocket. Arnold's pen scratched with erratic rhythm, punctuated periodically by the flopping noise of turning paper.

"Need your wet signature here, and how are you paying?" Arnold looked up at Iskander from his bent position over the paper-strewn desk.

"Actually, you better be paying cash. My wife's not here today and I don't know how to work the bank app."

"I've got cash." Iskander moved from the brochure stand to the desk and took up the pen.

"Full name here. Date here. Price paid here."

Arnold stabbed a narrow finger at blank spots on the page as he spoke, the sleeve of his starched shirt shining white under the domed office's lighting. Iskander filled in the spots and signed, and Arnold examined the form.

"Iskander Lotzki ... you're a UU kid?" Arnold said it like a question, but Iskander knew it was not.

"Lotzki is a common last name, it's not just for UU," he replied, in a voice so breezy and controlled that it almost gleamed with the polish of long practice. He copied Arnold's pronunciation, speaking each letter to sound out "you-you" instead of using the single, simple "oo" sound preferred by those who regularly interacted with the federal Unaccompanied Upbringing (UU) administration. The pronunciation switch was habitual among many kids raised in UU, and was even suggested in the UU career prep courses as a way to avoid correcting potential employers and colleagues.

Arnold regarded him for a few moments.

"But I'm right, aren't I? When there's a baby no one wants, they dump it to get raised in bulk by UU. With my taxes. And all those kids get the last name Lotzki."

"That'd be a stupid idea, to mark people out like that for their entire lives."

Iskander removed his wallet from his pocket and opened it.

"So, do I pay now or is there more for me to sign?"

Arnold stood for a moment, looking at him with papers held upright in his hands, before he spoke.

"Nope. Just hand over the cash and I'll sign over the deed. And I'll need to find the ig badge for you."

"No need, I found it in the lift."

Iskander pulled the five bills from his wallet and proffered them, hoping that Arnold would not press for a final visit to the now-functional lift and its highly-visible $4950 price tag. Arnold accepted the limp paper money and went to the back of the domed office, where a small safe was recessed into the floor. He knelt and pressed a button, eliciting a small but pleasant pinging noise from the safe. The door popped open and Arnold shuffled papers inside the safe for several seconds, emerging with a few cash bills and another, smaller touchscreen in his hands. As the safe door closed, it emitted a harsh honk.

Arnold presented the cash and the touchscreen to Iskander.

"Here's your change. Count it out and press your finger on the screen when you're done."

Iskander counted his change and pocketed the bills. He pressed his pointer finger against the touchscreen's surface, and the screen glowed green and vibrated.

Arnold pulled the touchscreen away and tapped at the controls.

"The deed is tied to your name now, but I don't have wireless here, so it won't show up on your personal right away. You'll get a paper copy in the mail in the next few days, too, but nobody cares about that except the government. You know how they love their paper."

Growing up, one of Iskander's minders had taught him to use a laminating machine to preserve and protect his birth papers. Seen as quaint on most other worlds, paper remained a reliable failsafe on Sargasso, where electronics routinely bricked themselves under the harsh electromagnetic skies.

Arnold eyed him appraisingly.

"So, you need me to move that lift for you, or not?"

Iskander shook his head.

"No thanks, I'll be okay."

Arnold opened his mouth to speak, but Iskander cut him off.

"I've got three hours to get it off the lot, right?"

Arnold closed his mouth, then sucked in a breath.

"It's tight quarters back there and just so you know, if you break something, you buy it. But yeah, you've got three hours."

He laid his touchscreen down, exchanging it for a thin sheaf of papers washed in a delicate pink, which he offered to Iskander.

"Here's your title."

Iskander took the sheets and folded them gently, then extended his hand to Arnold.

"Thanks."

"You're welcome. I don't want to see that thing on my lot when I get here tomorrow."

Late-afternoon sunlight spilled into the dim office as Iskander left with a grin on his face.

THE DAY'S light had aged to fat, heavy rays that mottled the cockpit with syrupy gold as Iskander sat in his new lift. The engine rumbled at its loping idle behind his back, and he grabbed the two protruding control sticks in the cockpit and pushed them up and down. The engine revved, beating faster through the firewall at his back as the lift supplied power to the massive steel arms outside the cab, following his movements on the control sticks. Iskander used the sticks to pantomime the simple up-and-down motions of lifting a cargo container, and grinned as he watched the lift's arms carry out his motions dutifully.

He eyed four pedals at his feet – two in the middle were flat and rectangular, while the two outer pedals were curved and had loose straps dangling from them. After several moments of study, Iskander gave one of them a quick, decisive tap with his foot.

The engine roared at his back and the lift lurched upward from its crouched parking stance. It was still for a moment, settled in an awkward half-crouch as Iskander stepped off the pedal, before the letters DAPR appeared in red on the dashboard. Unbidden, the machine corrected its precarious stance by surging fully upright so violently that Iskander was jerked in his seat harness.

Eyes wide, Iskander retrieved his personal from his pocket and tapped on the screen, inputting a search term as the engine wound back down to its loping idle.

Drive Assisting Posture Regulation (DAPR) detects dangerous deltas to center-of-gravity and automatically restores stability. DAPR also analyzes driver inputs on the controls and automatically moderates limb position and engine output to achieve the driver's intended motion. Drivers are discouraged from disabling DAPR before logging a minimum of 2,000 driving hours.

Iskander hovered his foot over the pedals again, swallowed, then gave one a steady press.

Behind him, the engine grumbled louder and the lift took a single, deliberate step forward, cockpit shaking as the leg landed at the end of its stride. He quickly stepped off the pedal, his lift halted, and the engine wound back down to idle.

Iskander blew several quick breaths in and out through pursed lips.

The derelict lifts around him cast long shadows in the late sun. He flicked on the lift's headlights, illuminating a stretch of open pathway that wound with gentle curves between the metal hulks. His bicycle's faded paint glowed blue, its frame hanging from one of the lift's forked manipulators in front of the headlights.

Iskander applied gentle pressure to the foot pedal, and the lift fell into an easy walk. He navigated the gigantic machine between its derelict neighbors, each turn guided by control sticks held in his white-knuckled grip. The cockpit bounced gently and not unpleasantly as the lift's heavy steel feet landed in the earth.

As he neared the lot's exit and began walking on pavement, the lift's feet stopped their rhythmic pounding and instead clacked pleasingly. Iskander relaxed in the seat, feeling secure inside the warm steel walls of the cockpit.

The street outside the lift lot was dusty and dark. Iskander steered onto the road and stepped harder on the throttle. His engine issued a measured growl that beat rhythmically against his back as the lift ambled forward into the night, headlights ablaze.

3 months before

DESPITE ITS enormous size, the approaching bus was quiet and swift. The noiseless grace of cars in motion had always been soothing for the young woman at the curb, but that same behavior was unsettling when wrapped in the steely bulk of a bus. She made herself stand at the curb affecting placid confidence, but as the bus drifted close and keened its pedestrian warning chime, a shot of nervous energy crackled through her feet, and she inched backward.

She waited at the curb just a few steps from her home, a row house with stone trim that had likely been tidy and attractive when it was built many, many years ago. Today, the home reeked of neglect. It was at least three different colors, all dulled by the sun, because its paint was peeling and revealing different coats of paint underneath, before that underlayer in turn peeled to reveal an even earlier hue. The stoop was halfway gone, since even concrete could rot under the right conditions. The home was squished against a dozen other row houses in a maze of blacktop streets and tall city buildings, separated from the urban scrum by only a sidewalk. Two alleyways, thin as razorblades, bracketed the row of houses on either side.

The only noticeable renovation of the past decade, or perhaps even the past several decades, was one-way privacy tint on the window glass, to allow the house's residents to see without the normal, fair exchange of being seen in return. The young woman at the curb had been a child when the tint was installed – tiny, hovering drones had draped the glass with blackened film while her mother smoothed it with squeegees, making a delicious rubbing sound. As she grew older, the young woman decided the one-way tint symbolized a kind of passive supervision toward who could see what, and it was how she first learned that privacy was a close cousin of control.

She straddled the line between adolescence and adulthood with a straight back and square, bony shoulders, face set in a carefully neutral expression, encouraging any observing gaze to pass over her. A close look, however, revealed eyes that boiled with watchfulness and a body that was held in a sort of calculated stillness, like an insect that felt itself watched by the slitted pupils of a predator, refusing any movement that might telegraph intent of its next maneuver.

Her uniform was black-speckled camouflage so recently removed from its packaging that it retained creases in the fabric, and she waited at the curb alone – it was traditional for friends and family to wait with new recruits, squeezing hands and speaking softly, but no one had volunteered and she could not bring herself to ask.

The air sat heavy and muggy above the sidewalk, beading sweat on her neck under the tall collar of her uniform, as she waited for the bus to stop. Once the huge vehicle was close, she was relieved to spot the friendly green paint of an access patch near the tall, recessed door. The bus rolled to a halt, and the only noise was the faint scrape of grit under its wheels and the keening of its low-speed pedestrian warning chime.

She stepped forward to press her personal against the access patch. Her hands betrayed her by shaking, smacking the frame of her personal against the bus's paint.

The door opened, revealing a bright stairwell with a crust of yellow paint on the ridges that rimmed each step. She began to climb. Her bag was a heavy, lumpy, sausage-shaped mass of military-green cloth, and it caught against the frame of the bus's door as she entered. The fabric was stretched taut around its contents – she was told she could bring anything she wanted, as long as it fit in the bag. She had taken this allowance to heart, knowing anything of value left behind could not be trusted to stay put. Moreover, she reasoned that the more she took now, the less reason she would have to come back.

With both hands, she heaved and slung the heavy bag over her shoulder, fitting at last into the doorway and mounting the remaining steps. As she climbed, she was met by a cool cascade of the bus's climate-controlled air, while the muggy air of her home city seemed to slough away, losing its grip on the fabric of her uniform as she disappeared inside the bus. She breathed deeply and looked down the aisle.

The bus interior was brightly lit by overhead bulbs, but utterly windowless, without even a windshield, as though she had stepped into the hull of a submarine rather than a bus. More than a dozen rows of bench seats extended from front to back and no driver was present, but a small, vestigial steering wheel and folding driver's seat were recessed near where she stood at the top of the steps.

Four other passengers occupied the benches, each sitting alone and spread at odd intervals throughout the bus's empty seats. All looked near her own age, all wore black-speckled camouflage uniforms, and all watched her in silence.

Her arms began to tremble from the weight of her densely-packed bag, and she lugged it a few rows back from the door and settled into an empty seat. A moment later, the bus accelerated.

The young man closest to her stood and leaned over the seatback between them, extending his hand.

"I'm Alfie, but my friend said nobody uses first names in the military, only last names, so I guess you call me Sandersenbach. Sorry in advance."

He grinned and she scanned his face carefully, while setting her own features into a familiar mask of diffident interest – not aloof enough to offend, but not focused enough to invite engagement.

Sandersenbach had a toothy smile and a scar bisecting one eyebrow with a thin track of hairless skin. What caught and held her gaze, however, was the collar of his uniform – the exact same black-speckled camouflage as her own.

No one on the bus, she realized, could see her home – looking around the interior, the windowless military bus could have been driving through the vacuum of space, for all that its occupants could see. For the first time that she could remember, a stranger like Sandersenbach was greeting her and not seeing worrying signs painted into her clothes, her belongings, and for long, humiliating stretches of her childhood, into the very smell of her unwashed skin.

Sandersenbach could see nothing but her uniform, and that was all she could see of him, in return. Everyone on the bus was a stranger of equal merit.

She reached over the tall seatback to shake his outreached hand.

"Eva," she said, and then hesitated. "Or, Sweetwater. Eva Sweetwater. It's nice to meet you."

Eva released his hand and withdrew into her seat, leaning against the wall of the bus. Sandersenbach sat back in his own seat and gestured to each of the bus's other passengers in turn.

"The sleeping one is Urobuchi. First name, Sayaka."

Sandersenbach indicated a young woman a few seats back who leaned against the bus's wall, eyes closed in what appeared to be deep slumber. Even in sleep her brow had wrinkles, as though it often furrowed out of concern or interest.

"The girl behind her is Weiss. I don't know her first name."

Sandersenbach did not have a quiet voice and Weiss was close enough to hear him, but she only stared into space, seemingly unaware that she was being discussed. She had removed her black-speckled camouflage shirt and folded it over her seatback, and the straps of a tank top undershirt rested on her smooth collarbones.

"I sure would like to know her first name!" Sandersenbach called, directing his words to Eva but raising his voice for Weiss. "Even though if she didn't want to tell me, that's okay, and I would respect that! I'm just curious! Is really all!"

Weiss flashed a brief glance at both of them.

"Yael," she said after a moment had passed, and then said nothing more.

Sandersenbach appeared delighted by this revelation, but he did not press Weiss any further, which Eva thought wise.

"Behind her is Ethan Talk," he said, returning his focus to Eva. "His last name is really easy to remember, because he actually doesn't say much."

Talk was visibly broad-shouldered, even under a layer of black camouflage fabric. He sat at the back of the bus, hands clasped in front of him and head bent as though deep in thought. His face was plainly constructed, lacking any particular feature that could be pointed out as unusual or striking, but the sum total was a profile of startling pleasantness. He looked up as Sandersenbach said his name and locked eyes with Eva. He gave her a wordless nod, and she replied with a small wave.

The bus motored onward in near silence. Eva was grateful for the quiet, although Sandersenbach was clearly restraining a powerful instinct to chat with everyone nearby. After a short while, the bus stopped braking and turning every few minutes, implying it had left the narrow streets near Eva's metropolitan home and was now trundling through longer, wider roads.

Hours passed. Urobuchi continued to sleep the day away and Eva made one fitful, unsuccessful attempt to doze before thumbing through the various social feeds on her personal, most of which she had already exhausted that morning while she waited for the bus. She slipped the personal's thin earbuds out of its frame and her fingernail found the pull tab of the expansion screen, tugging out the larger, papery display surface from the personal's frame and spreading it over her lap. On the bigger expansion screen, she watched two episodes of a drama about debaucherous politicians in ancient Persia-on-Earth while the bus barreled ever further into whatever blankness lay outside its sealed metal hull.

She was weighing the merits of braving the bus's narrow bathroom when the vehicle abruptly slowed, almost coming to a halt. A moment later, it swung a hard turn, and she grabbed the seatback in front of her for balance as the bus banged off the road. Something scraped against the hull outside, loud and threatening, and it took Eva a moment to realize it must be tree branches – the bus appeared to be laboring down a narrow, tree-lined road.

The floor rolled and pitched like a ship in heavy seas as the bus rumbled forward, each movement accompanied by a clang or a shaking panel on the interior. Eva's eyes stayed wide but she cautiously released the seatback in front of her as the bus made tortured but steady progress. Just as she leaned back and her head touched the cool vinyl seat, however, the bus must have hit a truly exceptional hole in the road because the entire vehicle tilted, knocking her head painfully into the seatback. A loud scraping noise from the undercarriage accompanied the sudden jerking, and Eva heard someone let out a yelp. The bus's engine whirred and it lurched out of the hole, jerking its passengers in their seats and sending many of their sausage-like bags tumbling.

Urobuchi awoke at the bus's jarring and blinked blearily at the scene, eventually fixating on her bag, which had been stored in an overhead rack and was now splayed flaccidly over the top of a nearby seatback. She stood and pulled the bag to her, stuffing it into the corner between the seat and the wall. She gave the bus a once over and scratched her cheek, nodding acknowledgement to Eva, a newcomer for her concern, before laying down across her seat using the bag as a pillow. Within moments, she appeared fast asleep again.

Talk's bag had also been stored overhead and burst open when it fell, spewing clothing and bottled personal care items that rolled out of reach under the seats.

Although she had remained inert for the majority of the bus ride, the girl in the white tank top, Weiss, was suddenly in motion, possibly capitalizing on her proximity to Talk, his broad shoulders, and his time of need.

She leaned hard under nearby seats to grab at his rolling bottles as they zipped across the bus's gritty floor, while Talk offered quiet thanks and she responded with enthusiastic graciousness. Sandersenbach observed this interaction, somewhat intensely, from several seats away.

The bus lurched again, slowing as it entered another rut, but this time Eva was prepared with her back tucked into the corner of her seat and knee braced against the seatback in front. The bus groaned and scraped its way out of the dip with a series of ghastly noises and lurching movements, and this time all five of its passengers kept their bags beside them, secure.

3 months before

HOURS LATER, Eva sank into a restless and unsatisfying sleep on the bus's narrow bench seat. When she awoke, an occasional dip or rumble from below her seat confirmed that the bus still traveled on rough roads, but the bus ride was otherwise unchanged – the air was still cool, the lighting was still bright, and the passenger count was unchanged.

She stood, stretched, and wondered when they would be given more food – containers of packaged snacks and drinks had unlocked at the front of the bus around the fourth or fifth hour of driving, but her personal showed the time as early morning, meaning it had been almost a dozen hours since she had a full meal.

The bus abruptly applied its brakes, slapping Eva's hip against the seatback in front. Sighs, yawns, smacking of lips, and other small awakening noises from the bus's other occupants peppered the interior as the bus came to a complete stop in the road.

Several minutes later, the bus's door opened and a woman climbed the stairwell with booted thumps. She stopped at the top of the steps and folded her arms, looking down the bus's long, narrow interior.

Her uniform was the same as Eva and her bus-mates – speckled black camouflage. She was not tall enough to be imposing through height alone, but her jaw was strong and her expression was flat, bordering on grim, with her hair contained in a ruthlessly tidy bun. The soft roundness of pregnancy pressed out against the fabric at her midriff, and her demeanor was one of implacable military sternness. More than anything else, though, Eva thought the woman looked tired.

Her gaze rested on Eva first.

"Sweetwater."

She said Eva's surname with stern authority, and only after a moment had passed did Eva realize the statement had been a question.

She nodded quickly, and the woman's gaze shifted behind Eva.

"Sandersenbach. Urobuchi. Weiss. Talk."

There was a faint pause between each name, just enough for each passenger to nod at their time.

The woman's arms were still folded.

"Your applications to join the Special Operations and Oversight group, commonly known as soot group, have been provisionally accepted. You have arrived at Camp Albatross, a soot group training facility. If you complete your boot-strapping here, you will be immediately granted the rank of Specialist and your mandatory term of service will be reduced to two years. If you fail, you will return to the general Navy and complete boot-strapping elsewhere as a Private First Class, then go on to a normal three-year tour."

Each statement was delivered like a paper cutter, slicing neatly.

"I am Chief Warrant Officer Marko. You may not see me again for some time, but if you are successful here at Camp Albatross, I will be your reporting officer. Good luck."

Chief Marko turned without another word and walked down the bus's steps. The door hissed close behind her, and Eva exchanged looks with the other passengers.

Minutes passed, and Eva's stomach rumbled as she settled into her seat and kept her bag close. The bus hummed, pushing cool air through its vents, keeping them in unobtrusive comfort. Urobuchi and Sandersenbach made quiet conversation as the minutes stretched, and Urobuchi eventually left her seat to poke at the bus's door. It did not open, despite her massaging, and she returned with a shrug.

Eva checked her personal, which noted that 43 minutes had passed since the bus stopped moving. Her thumb tapped on the screen to check her location, but the personal's map was a sea of featureless green. She pinched the screen and saw no towns or even buildings nearby – if they had arrived at a training facility, it was hidden from the maps on Eva's personal.

A sudden clack signaled that the bus's door was opening once again. This time, it was a squat, powerfully-built man climbing the stairs, wearing the same speckled black camouflage uniform. A pistol clung to one hip, and a long, glossy baton to the other.

After several quiet seconds, the man cleared his throat.

"Welcome to Camp Albatross, recruits. Grab your bags and line up outside."

As the passenger closest to the door, Eva was first in line and she clutched her bag to her chest, making herself as small as possible to fit in the thin gap between the man and the bus's stairway. Outside the bus's doorway, the sky was dim, but she could make out trees in the distance across an open field of close-cut grass. The air was hot and soggy with moisture, spreading a clammy film across her nose and cheeks, stinking of warm mud.

Once all of the bus's occupants had filed out of the doorway, the man with the pistol and the baton produced a personal from his pocket and tapped a few times on its display. The bus's door closed automatically and it began to reverse, backing down the road from which it came.

"Make sure you've got your bag, and follow me," said the man. "I hope you all slept when you had the chance."

Eva swallowed, hitched her dull green bag up onto her shoulders, and stepped into the wet grass to follow him.

3 months before

EVA'S HANDS shook when she lifted her fork.

There were no seats, so she sat on the floor against a wall. A metal plate on her lap was hot from the food heaped on it, and the plate's warmth soaked into her thighs. The heat was pleasant, but every other piece of her was miserable.

Dinner was potatoes laced with protein syrup, and vegetables cooked soft and grainy with salt on top. Unappetizing, but she had eaten worse. Moreover, the food was steaming hot and she could eat as much as she wanted – these two benefits were not lost on Eva, who had spent most of her life stretching one school lunch into the next. Arriving at homeroom without breakfast and leaving school with little expectation of dinner, she used to loiter near the counter where students dropped off trays after lunch, swiping leftovers and marveling at the other kids' waste – entire bananas, perfectly yellow and unpeeled, or untouched squeeze packs of hummus and peanut butter that gave a wonderful crack as you twisted the cap. Sometimes entire sandwiches, still in shiny packaging with clear windows to see inside, where the plastic beaded with moisture.

She ate an enormous forkful of pasty cauliflower and a smudge caught in the crease of her mouth, as the fork tines were poorly guided by her trembling hands. The shaking in her limbs couldn't come from fear or anger, since all emotion had fled her body hours earlier, shoved aside by the unbearable burden of surviving the day. Instead, the tremors came from muscles stressed far beyond their capacity – every piece of her ached, from her calves to her neck.

She hadn't done a push-up since gym class, which became an elective after sophomore year and one she immediately elected to drop, but today she had done two hundred. Or rather, their drill instructor – a man with bushy eyebrows named Motty – had counted out two hundred push-ups in bursts over the course of the day, alongside hundreds of repetitions of other body-weight exercises. Exactly how many repetitions she had completed was uncertain, but it had not been enough to please him.

From the moment she and her bus-mates left the dirt road, Motty had ordered them through an endless string of exercise in the mud and grass, and her new uniform became smeared with vegetation and dirt. She had tried to spare her green, sausage-like bag by setting it aside, and fury bubbled in her chest when she later found it rolled into a watery mud patch nearby. A moment later, however, Motty had screamed for more push-ups, and her rage evaporated as her arms shook, popped, and finally failed to keep her up off the rich-smelling wet grass.

Next it had been lunges, or squats, or clambering over tires and under low-slung ropes. Motty took an obvious pleasure in pushing them past their limits, and he often tailored the number of sets and repetitions to them on an individual level – if Eva was told to do a set of twenty, one of her bus-mates might receive a set of fifteen. Perhaps Motty had reviewed the data on their physicals beforehand, or maybe he just assessed their worth on-the-fly with eyes and intellect like a cracking whip – Eva had stopped caring about the how or why, and focused only on grunting through her repetitions fast enough to avoid a hard poke or slap from Motty's baton.

The thought of doing it all tomorrow made her want to weep. Instead, she forked a mouthful of potato and chewed.

She was in a low cement building, seated on a scuffed tile floor in some sort of lobby. There was no furniture aside from an empty, chair-less reception desk, the table piled with warm, flavorless nutrition, and plates and forks to shovel it with. Her bus-mates were scattered around the room, and most ate silently with blank stares. What little conversation there was occurred in indistinct mutters until the girl in the white tank top, Weiss, appeared next to her.

"Hi."

Her voice sounded oddly small.

"I'm sorry he made you carry my bag this morning. It was my mistake, not yours."

If all the humor inside her hadn't been burned for fuel hours earlier, Eva might have laughed. She had forgotten the scene completely – Weiss had made some imaginary infraction and as punishment, Motty forced Eva to carry Weiss's bag, as well as Eva's own, for several running laps. The scene had felt banal and tropey even then – Motty turned it into a heavy-handed parable about mistakes on the battlefield having unforeseen consequences – but Eva felt a flicker of warmth toward the thin, mud-spattered girl squatting next to her, using legs that must be exploding with pain at the effort, to say she was sorry.

Eva shook her head.

"Motty was just setting us up so he could give that little speech. If it wasn't you, it would've been the next person to make some tiny mistake."

Weiss smiled with gratitude, then spoke quietly.

"It fucking sucks here."

Eva nodded in emphatic agreement.

"I'm going to feel better if I cry. I don't need to—" Weiss stopped to glance at Eva's face, "—but I want to, so I'm going to find a bathroom or something. Do you want to come with me?"

Something turned inside Eva, unlocking, and a hurricane of dismay twisted in her chest. Her fork clanked against the metal plate and Weiss grabbed her hand, squeezing hard. Together, they stood, bracing one another as their abused muscles protested standing upright, and pushed toward a door at the back of the room. The third girl, Urobuchi, met Eva's eyes as they passed. Eva shot out her hand and Urobuchi took it without a word, clambering stiffly to her feet.

Without a word to their bus-mates, the trio pushed through a door at the back of the room.

The lobby was connected to a larger building by a narrow hallway, where the windows were blackened by night outside and the lighting was dim. Eva, Weiss, and Urobuchi had no sooner turned the nearest corner than they came up short, nearly running into a pregnant woman in a black-speckled uniform, who regarded them with weary surprise.

"Where are you going?"

Chief Warrant Officer Marko's voice held no annoyance, or any emotion at all besides curiosity, but the quiet gravity of her presence was intimidating.

"We were looking for someplace away from the others," Weiss said.

"Why?"

"Just to sit."

"And do what?"

"Be alone." Weiss hesitated. "Together."

Chief Marko studied them wordlessly, her eyes black and featureless in the hallway's poor lighting. If she came to any understanding or realization, she didn't show it, but when she spoke Eva thought her tone had softened.

"There's a private bathroom two doors down, on the left. The door sticks but give it a good shove and it'll open. Be back in the meal room in ten minutes."

"Yes, Chief."

"Wait."

Chief Marko glanced side to side before she spoke again, confirming their solitude in the dim hallway. In anyone else, the gesture could have been furtive. In Chief Marko, it seemed only a calm gathering of information rightly needed.

"It's good that you're together – keep doing that. You three should stick close, and keep tabs. Do you understand?"

Eva was not certain she did understand, but she, Weiss, and Urobuchi nodded silently. Chief Marko returned their stares for another moment before giving them a nod.

"Ten minutes, then back in the meal room."

"Yes, Chief."

ISKANDER HIT the park button on his lift's dashboard and waited, bracing against the armrest as the cockpit straightened with a small jolt and the lift's legs bent into a crouched parking stance. As he climbed out the side door, cheerful rays of morning sun glinted on the steely limbs and glazed windshields of other lifts in the parking lot.

Iskander straightened after climbing down to the pavement and rubbed the arms of his coat for warmth. The zipper on his coat was stuck inoperable and the flaps hung open, letting in gulps of morning chill that the sun had not yet burned away.

Behind a low administrative building, stacks of shipping containers rose several dozen feet in the air. The containers had blunt pointed ends but were square enough to be stacked, and were painted in dull, industrial hues. Through small gaps between the towers of containers, Iskander glimpsed the tall silhouettes of lifts, windshields glinting as they walked.

A sign at the entrance read "Picochee County Orbital Freight Handling Facility" – from his reading, Iskander knew it was colloquially known as the Picochee mitt, with "mitt" being parlance for any orbital shipping facility that caught cargo dropped from orbit. There was a mitt every few hundred miles on Sargasso, with each catching their respective region's overspace freight.

Mitts were also responsible for hurling exported freight from the ground up to orbit. Small amounts of cargo could be mailed express using the same air-conditioned, noise-dampened passenger shuttles that ferried citizens between worlds, but that shipping was only for the most valuable, fragile, or time-sensitive packages.

For as long as humans had reached their hands to space, some equations had never changed – every ounce of cargo had to be dragged upward through mile after mile of empty sky, burning fuel and fighting gravity for each inch of altitude, before finally reaching the weightlessness of space. The expensive, explosive rockets of early spaceflight might be ancient history, but the physics of the problem were timeless.

Therefore, exporting the ponderous freight of everyday life – cartons of milk, ceramic floor tiles, bulk rice, charcoal briquettes – on a fuel-burning shuttle to space was simply too costly, and the slower, cheaper freight-gun shipping network, powered by facilities like the Picochee mitt, was the only feasible choice.

In the distance behind the stacks of shipping containers, a freight-gun launch track rose from the ground, a fat ribbon of black steel that climbed dizzyingly high before terminating, a ramp to empty air. The ramp was anchored at its lower end but had no support along its narrow length, instead being suspended by jaw-droppingly massive and colorful balloons – some verdant green, others a furious red, each of them large enough to blot out the sun. Large panels, shining white plastic or fiberglass a bit like the sails on a boat, hung down below the floating end of the ramp. Working in tandem with gas pressure in the leviathan balloons that raised and lowered the ramps at will, or even settled them on the ground during foul weather, the plastic sails caught wind to aim the tip of the ramp at the behest of the mitt's shipping computer.

Below the metal ramp, the elevated track for the freight-gun stretched in a gentle arc, forming a circle several miles across and studded along its circumference with more ramped launch tracks. As Iskander watched, one of the drab shipping containers sped by with a clatter of noise, accelerated along the track like a cart on a roller coaster, building up enormous speed so slowly along miles of circular steel railway that its cargo was barely jostled by the acceleration. At the right time, the right split-second moment when the one container among many was at speed, and the wind rested easy between gusts, and there was minimal cloud or rain to obfuscate the container's path, then a computer would shunt it from the track. The container would be launched with enormous velocity, up and away from one of the tall, thin launch ramps that ballooned themselves aloft.

Achieving orbit in space solely via launch from the freight-gun ramps was impractical – the energy required would smash all but the sturdiest cargo. The launch from the ramp was a good start, however, hurling the containers high above the clouds, where they could be caught by one of the superlow-orbit handling platforms that dotted Sargasso's sky. These platforms hung from tethers connected to a second freight facility still miles higher, in true orbit. Both facilities combined were a thousand times less costly than an orbital elevator or shuttle fleet, and the electricity that accelerated the containers along the tracks was practically free, allowing overspace shipments to be piped cheaply to space.

To Iskander, however, the business of getting cargo to space was immaterial – he was here for cargo *from* space. In the nearby sky, dark specks plummeted straight down from the heavens toward the center of the launch track. The area was pockmarked with huge pneumatic catching pits that stretched deep underground to safely dissipate the enormous velocity of inbound shipping containers, which were shoved with the barest ceremony off the orbital handling platforms. It was this inbound cargo, falling specks in the sky filled with vacuum cleaners or electronics or artisan cheese, which brought Iskander and his lift to the parking lot of the Picochee mitt.

Nearby, a large sign read "day work" while another sign read "hourly work." Each sign crested a different doorway into the same low, rust-colored building – the only building on the mitt, from what Iskander could see.

He studied the day and hourly work signs as he crossed the parking area, having never seen these two categories of work mentioned in his studies. As he passed the simple rope fence that separated car parking from lift parking and neared the low brown building, he slowed, hesitating between the two signs, before finally pushing through the door for hourly work with a slight shrug.

The office inside was warm but not stuffy, and small without feeling cramped. Flowers cascaded out of pots near the windows, draping the plain fiberboard walls in extravagant color backed by leaves of vibrant, plump green. The seats that lined the walls were upholstered in delicate lavender that matched the trim on the walls and ceiling, and a small but cheerful water fountain tinkled nearby.

The pleasant space was empty, save for a woman behind a desk at the back of the office. She looked up as Iskander entered, slender eyebrows knit in surprise. As he approached, she pressed one finger against her lips and the crisp white cuffs of her shirt brushed her chin, bracelets tinkling.

With her other hand, she pointed behind her, and Iskander saw a very young boy, only 2 or 3 years old, fast asleep behind her desk. He lay on a small cot, in the center of a hurricane of colored blankets.

Iskander smiled impulsively, and pressed his own finger to his lips in acknowledgement as he approached the woman with soft steps.

When he was close enough, she addressed him in a whisper that did nothing to distract from her effortless certainty.

"You're in the wrong place."

Iskander froze, his smile slipping.

"This is the office for hourly workers," she continued, still in a whisper. "You need a badge to come in through here, but you don't have one. I know, because only I give them out. You want the day laborer's office, next door."

Iskander planted a wry grin on his face.

"Sorry, this is my first time here," he whispered.

The woman smiled back politely.

"Well, welcome to the Picochee mitt. You have a lift, or are you looking for hand work?"

"I have a lift, ma'am."

The boy on the cot stirred, making a soft mumbling sound, and the woman waited until he had quieted before continuing to whisper to Iskander.

"Head next door and Rico will sort you out. The line will be mostly hand workers by this time, though, and I'm not sure how many lift jobs will be left. Drivers start lining up at five. Not everyone gets here that early, but you get the good jobs if you do."

"Five in the morning?" Iskander kept his tone *sotto voce* but could not keep the shock from his face.

The woman nodded firmly.

"Might want to hurry over there," she whispered.

Iskander nodded and walked to the exit, treading softly in his boots. He paused short of opening the door to wallow for a moment in the smell of lavender and other small, pleasant herbs suffusing the air. He turned toward her desk, his hand still on the door handle.

"Did you do all this?" he asked, softly.

His free hand gestured at the thriving plants, tasteful furniture, and delicious-smelling air.

"I did," she said.

Iskander paused.

"It's really nice in here," he replied at last, and she cocked her head appreciatively.

"Well, thank you," she whispered. "I spend a lot of time behind this desk."

Iskander nodded a little wistfully and left.

A harsh winter wind outside stole warmth from inside his coat as he crossed the short patch of cracked pavement to the door of the day laborer's office.

He pushed on the door, but it thumped against an unseen barrier and refused to complete its swing. Iskander pushed again, more gently, and this time the door creaked fully open with a series of loud, metallic twangs. The barrier, it turned out, had been a large man in denim overalls. His hair was cropped close but uneven, displaying irregular thickets of hair, dandruff, and scalp. He regarded Iskander wordlessly, the last person in a line of men and women crowded into the office. They were all workers in heavy coats and sturdy boots, filling the room to capacity and organized into a line by thin, haggard-looking rope dividers. The pale fiberboard walls bore streaks of dark grime near the floorboards, and the air smelled of warm human skin. The space was almost gratuitously dingy, as though it sought to offset the neighboring office's delicate charm.

The end of the rope divider corralling the workers was capped with a small, battered sign. Faded writing and an arrow tremulously declared the start of the line for day workers, but the queue extended well past it, ending with the man in overalls who had blocked the door – he had shuffled to the side after Iskander entered and was now blocking the door again. Iskander lined up behind him.

Minutes ticked by as Iskander waited in line, periodically shuffling forward a few steps as the line moved. Workers left out the door behind Iskander, some moving with purpose, others traipsing dejectedly. No one came in to line up behind Iskander, and without warning, the large man in front of Iskander loudly passed wind. Iskander shuffled a few steps back and the man muttered an indistinct apology.

Iskander checked his personal again. He had advanced perhaps one-third of the way into the line, and his stomach was beginning to grumble.

A full hour after he had arrived, Iskander's eyed bored into the back of the large, flatulent man, willing him to greater haste as he plodded forward from his place in line toward the small window at the front of the office.

The large man spoke in mutters to the person behind the window, and papers were shuffled back and forth. At length, he lumbered back from the window and proceeded with thumping footsteps to the door, banging it shut behind him as he left. The flimsy rope dividers now corralled only empty space, and Iskander alone remained in line. He breathed a sigh and approached the counter.

A broad, brushed steel shelf offered space for paperwork, jutting out from the glass that walled off the office behind it. The glass was privacy fogged, revealing only the silhouette of the clerk behind it. Iskander stepped up the glass, cleared his throat, and tried to remember the key words he had read about freelance lift work.

"Hi, I'm looking for some—"

"—you're still here!"

A cheerful voice behind the glass interrupted Iskander, and he looked up from his papers. Up close, the glass was almost transparent, and the woman from the hourly office was regarding him with amusement.

"I thought you worked the other office," he said, smiling.

"I work this desk every once in a while, if Rico needs a break. It was a long line today, but I guess you already know that. I thought you'd have given up and gone home."

"Can't do that," Iskander shook his head. "I need to start today."

She nodded, but her mouth twisted with concern as she scanned a display in front of her.

"We don't have much left for lift work, but let's see."

She tapped her finger a few times on the screen.

"Name?"

"Iskander Lotzki."

"Nice to meet you, I'm Paulette." She spoke distractedly as she clicked and scrolled through screens on the display in front of her. "What's your GLC?"

Iskander chewed his lip.

"Gross lifting class. Some people call it a picking bracket?" she supplied helpfully.

Iskander shook his head.

"I'm sorry, I don't know."

Paulette's eyes narrowed, and the humor in them began to fade.

"Nip dexterity?"

Iskander shook his head again.

"I'm going to guess – no license?"

There was a faint edge in her voice now, and when she finished speaking, her lips pressed into a flat line.

Iskander shook his head.

"So, what did you expect to happen today?"

The sudden and intense disdain in her voice was rattling. Iskander placed his hands flat on the shelf and tried to look harmless.

"I read that a license isn't technically required and I just – I was thinking I could get a little bit of work today and learn as I went."

Paulette tapped on her screen, not meeting his eyes. Iskander could hear her fingernail click hard against the screen.

"I do not allow unlicensed drivers on my mitt – picking freight is dangerous enough without unlicensed drivers making it worse. You've got a lift, so you, or whoever bought it for you, can clearly afford to pay for school. You come in here with the proper knowledge and the proper papers, or you don't come at all. Please leave."

Iskander's head drooped. The earlier growls in his stomach had turned to hard-edged hunger pangs as he waited in line. He began calculating the hours left in the day – the open job calls at the Picochee community center would have ended by now.

"I'm sorry, ma'am. I didn't mean to offend you."

"I'm not offended – you just can't work here."

Iskander scraped his papers off the brushed steel shelf. His empty stomach gnawed at him, and he did his best to keep his back straight.

"Do you have any other jobs?"

Paulette's eyes went flinty and he heard her suck in a breath.

"I just told you—"

"—no, no, I mean … I'm sorry I interrupted you, but—" Iskander put his hands up in apology and bowed his head, "—I just meant, do you have any other work? *Not* driving a lift."

She studied him irritably but said nothing. After a moment of silence, Iskander blew out a breath and tapped his fist dejectedly on the steel shelf.

"You mentioned hand work earlier, and I'm not sure what that means, but maybe I can do that. Or even … I could do some cleaning."

He looked around at the sparsely appointed waiting room.

"Maybe I could clean in here. Or if there's bathrooms, I'll clean those. Just, some job that needs doing but nobody wants to do it. I'm okay with electrics and machines, I could take a look at that lighting panel up there."

He pointed above them to a panel that flickered at odd intervals.

"No job is too small or too grim for me, ma'am. And I'll leave, of course, if you don't have anything for me. But before I go, I just wanted to … check."

"Where did you get your lift?"

A new woman's voice came from close behind Iskander, startling him. He had not heard the door to the waiting area open, and the voice had an accent he could not place. He felt compelled to answer, and quickly.

"Arnold's Lift Lot, over in Attowa."

"You live out there?"

The woman had a strong, strange accent, but her syllables were crisp. Her jumpsuit was drab but spotless, worn with the top half off her sinewy shoulders, sleeves tied tight around the waist. Her age was hard to pinpoint, with strong shadows drawn on her skin from the smoked ceiling lights of the waiting room, but he guessed she had at least twenty years on him.

"No, I just went there to get the lift."

The woman in the jumpsuit nodded, while Paulette sat silently behind the glass barrier of the clerk's desk. She seemed to be studying their conversation and Iskander noted that at least for now, she was no longer ordering him to leave.

"Why do you want to work at this mitt?" the woman in the jumpsuit asked.

"I don't, really, but I don't mean that rudely," he said. "I only chose this mitt because I live nearby. I just want to work."

Iskander hesitated, and felt heat rise in his face. As of that morning, he had a negative balance of funds in his account.

"But, it would be good if I could work here, for today. At least today."

The woman in the jumpsuit used an elbow to push out of her lean against the wall.

"Let me see one of your boots," she said.

Iskander glanced at Paulette, but she only sat mute, observing from behind the glass.

"You want my boots?"

"Just one. Please take it off."

Iskander turned again to look questioningly at Paulette.

"Don't look at me, she's the one asking," Paulette said, her stare still hard and unfriendly.

Iskander knelt and began to remove one of his boots. His socks were sweaty, and the cool of the tile floor seeped through the fabric as he handed his boot to the woman in the jumpsuit.

She turned it over in her hands, not seeming to mind the grime on the sole that flaked off on her fingers. As she inspected his boot, Iskander saw that her own looked sturdy. Their leather was worn but clean, and the laces were new, and tied tightly.

"Thank you," she handed him back his boot. "How many pairs of shoes do you own?"

"What? Why does that matter?"

The woman in the jumpsuit did not reply, only stared at him expectantly, and Iskander did not dare to glance at Paulette again.

"A few, I guess? Five or six? I don't know exactly – just a normal number of shoes." Iskander felt his face beginning to warm again.

"You can't be more specific?"

He hesitated, and the woman continued.

"Please take a moment and think carefully. How many pairs of shoes do you own?"

Iskander wanted to raise his hands and make a show of counting on his fingers, but the woman in the jumpsuit held his gaze, and his hands stayed at his side. Humiliatingly, he felt a sudden lump in his throat.

"Just these boots, ma'am," he said, keeping his face very still. "One pair."

"Can you bend and lift 15 kilos?"

"Yes, ma'am."

"Can you do at least one pullup?"

"Yes, ma'am."

"Please show me your hands."

Iskander presented his hands and the woman gripped them, turning them over and back for inspection. Her fingers felt hard and warm, and her nails were clean.

"What's this?" she asked, pointing to large, purple splotches on his palms and fingers.

"Blackberry juice. I'm a picker, when they're in season."

"Farms don't have machines for that?"

"Not blackberries or raspberries, they're too fragile. Even with hand-picking, a lot get mushed and end up as jam or preserves."

She released his hands and digested this information wordlessly for several seconds before directing her voice toward the glass behind him.

"Let me take him for today, Paulette. There's a slop truck coming by – I'll show him the ropes and he can work down there all week, by himself. Only thing that'll get hurt is his sense of smell."

Behind the glass, Paulette gave a loud sniff.

"Is he your next stray?" she asked.

"Already looking for another one?" The woman in the jumpsuit grinned as she spoke, and Paulette giggled.

Iskander smiled hesitantly, but both women ignored him.

"Well ..." Paulette drew out the word as she considered. "... he did stand in line behind Dan this whole time."

The woman in the jumpsuit made an indistinct noise, but it sounded vaguely pitying.

"Stinky Dan?" she asked.

"Stinky Dan," Paulette confirmed. "All right, but he doesn't set one toe outside that pit until he's got the hours."

"Not one toe, Paulette. Not even his littlest one."

Paulette giggled again and Iskander heard her chair rolling backward. Behind the glass, she faded to a silhouette, then disappeared.

The woman in the jumpsuit shifted her weight on her hip and regarded Iskander for several long moments.

"You're welcome," she said at last, somewhat dryly.

Iskander started.

"Sorry ... thank you."

He paused and behind the glass, the sound of the rolling chair floated out to him a second time as Paulette reappeared in the window.

The woman in the jumpsuit cleared her throat at Iskander, and he moved to the side. She leaned past him, her fingers finding the edges of a long, fat brown envelope that Paulette had slipped through a slot in the glass enclosure.

"Can you get good me a good deal on blackberries?"

It took Iskander a moment to realize that Paulette was speaking to him.

"Sure," he said. "About half what you'd pay at the grocery, and fresher, too."

"I'd like a full pound, and drop them off tomorrow morning *before* you go down to the slop. I'll reimburse you in your pay – money goes out on Friday."

Iskander swallowed. He had been hoping for daily pay, but his rent was in good standing, so Friday was doable if he was creative about what constituted a meal. The chair rolled back away from the glass once more, and Paulette was gone for good.

"Let's go and see what kind of lift driver you are," said the woman in the jumpsuit.

"So, you're helping me?" Iskander tried to keep suspicion out of his tone.

The woman watched him out of the corner of her eye as she tucked the brown envelope from Paulette into a pocket of her jumpsuit.

"That was my intent." Her voice had a wry lilt.

Iskander's expression was guarded, while the woman's face was patient.

"You won't owe me any money, or favors, or anything at all. Every once in a while, I just try to help when I see that help's needed – that's all. You're welcome to come outside and show me how you drive, or I can go to lunch and you can head over to another mitt. You won't hurt my feelings either way."

His stomach grumbled, and he hoped she could not hear.

"Okay," he said, after several moments of thought. "Thank you."

"You're welcome. And I'm sorry about before – pressing you on how many shoes you own. I think it helped to soften Paulette up, but there are probably kinder ways I could have handled that. So, I'm sorry."

Iskander watched her carefully, looking for any sign of insincerity, but found none.

"That's all right," he said at last. "Thank you for … intervening. How did you know I only have the one pair?"

"I didn't." She shrugged agreeably. "Come on outside."

She turned on her heel toward the exit. Iskander followed, then turned and ran back to the shelf to grab his papers before hustling back to the door, which had already closed behind her and shuttered him in the gloom of the waiting area.

THE MIDDAY air was warm and pleasant, having lost the morning chill while Iskander queued in the hourly work office line. He removed his coat and tucked it under his arm, falling into step next to the woman in the jumpsuit.

"So, what's your name?" she asked.

"Iskander."

"Nice to meet you, Iskander. I'm assuming that's your name, not your lift's callsign?"

"That's right. I don't think I have a callsign – this is my first day."

"You have one, but its either random nonsense from the factory, or whatever the last owner coded in there. Around the mitt, drivers tend to go by their lift's callsign, not their own name. There's a decent number of siblings and married couples at this mitt …" She paused to gesture at the distant stacks of shipping containers, and the numerous lifts at work behind them. "… so callsigns prevent confusion between sites and shift assignments. My callsign is Ruin."

Iskander blinked, and Ruin laughed.

"I didn't pick it, but it stuck. Pick yours soon, or someone will pick it for you. No more than three syllables and no profanity."

"Yes, ma'am," he nodded.

"So, how'd you wind up with a lift, but no lift license, Iskander?"

"I read that licenses are only needed for the drivers down below the mitt, at the bottom of the catching pits – drivers on the surface aren't supposed to need them. Then I found a lift that runs at a good price, and I saw that Picochee offers freelance surface work, so I figured I'd show up and learn by doing."

"But how did you learn to drive a lift, without the licensing courses?"

"Well … I'm sort of self-taught. I watched a lot of videos, and I found some night classes for licensure that would let me audit the first few days for free. I got a copy of the textbook, and I found some exam samples on the feed and passed them."

Ruin was giving him an odd look, and he swallowed.

"I know I don't have the *practical* driving experience from the courses, but I'm really good on the theory, at least."

"I'm not sure there's much theory to grasp on the topic of stacking cans, but I'm pleased to hear that you did your homework."

Her tone was dry, but amused, and Iskander felt a tinge of relief mix with his anxiety.

"I know it's not the conventional path," he paused and swallowed. "But it took a really long time for me to save up, and then I got lucky finding my lift at the price it was. Now that I've got it, I need to get to work. Soon. Really soon."

"Fair enough," Ruin said. "You're not wrong about the licenses. Surface drivers don't technically need them, but mitt bosses like Paulette are free to set their own rules and require them anyway. The good news for you is that even if you don't take a licensing course, once you log eighty hours of driving time without accidents on an accredited mitt like Paulette's, you can apply to have the license granted automatically."

Iskander pondered this information quietly.

"So, who *wouldn't* have a license? Besides me?"

Ruin hummed as she considered.

"Not many people. Generally the folks that put money into buying a lift either have the license already, or can pay for the course. Eighty hours without accidents isn't easy if you're new to driving, so the courses are still a good option and they don't cost that much, compared to the lift."

She cast Iskander a sidelong glance. "Usually."

The lift parking lot was now empty except for Iskander's green-and-black Model 49, crouched in its parking stance. Iskander and Ruin stood in the shade it cast from the late morning sun, and she eyed his lift appraisingly.

"How much did you pay for this?"

Iskander hesitated.

"No judgement, I'm just trying to get the lay of the land here," she said.

"Almost five thousand, out the door. But the seller didn't know that the engine worked, so it might be worth more."

Ruin nodded with a grunt that Iskander could not attach an emotion to.

"And it runs well?"

"Ran all the way from Attowa. I stopped to eat once, and it started right up again."

Ruin squinted at Iskander.

"When did you buy it?" she asked.

"Late yesterday. Then I came straight here, didn't even go home."

Iskander had intended the statement to prove his diligence, but it only made Ruin squint at him even more confusedly.

"Why did it take you all night to get here from Attowa?"

"It wasn't the whole night, more like ten hours. I mean, a lift only walks so fast, right?"

A burst of giggles from Ruin startled him. Her eyes were creased into merry arcs as the tiny, friendly laugh played oddly against her cool demeanor.

"So, when you say 'ran', you mean the *engine* ran. But you *walked* it from Attowa?"

Iskander felt heat creep up from his neck to fill the skin of his cheeks. He was unsure why he should be embarrassed, which made it more embarrassing.

"So ..." Ruin paused and fanned herself with her hand, "... you were in soft-step gear. It's the lowest gear, basically a safety gear that forces the lift to walk slowly. On highways, lifts stick to the dirt on the side of the road, and they run, so the trip from Attowa should normally take ... mmm ... *not* ten hours. Climb up, and I'll show you."

With one hand, Ruin gestured to Iskander to climb the steps of his lift, while her other hand covered her mouth. The corners of a smile peeked out from behind her fingers, but there was no harshness in her face as she regarded him, features shadowed by the bulk of his lift's frame.

Iskander smiled back wanly and placed his boot on the bottom rung of his lift's access ladder, vaulting up to the cockpit and slipping into the side door. Ruin climbed up behind him and swung up onto the roof. She knocked on the top hatch, and Iskander unlocked it as he settled himself into the cockpit's seat. Ruin lifted the top hatch, its hinge emitting a variety of twangs like the screen door to a neglected, rain-damp porch. Ruin peered inside the cockpit from above, and Iskander reached for the ACC POWER button.

"Hang on, let me get settled up here," she said.

Iskander rested the heel of his palm of the dusty dashboard, fingers hovering, eager to convey his readiness to strike at the many buttons and dials.

"Okay," she said at last. "Hit the accessory power."

Iskander tapped the button, and the dashboard flickered to life, gauges whirling and lights twinkling. A few moments passed and the displays calmed, keeping only the bright green START CHECK illuminated.

"Looks good so far, but hold off on starting it. Check continuity on each limb."

Iskander hesitated.

"That little picture over your head." Ruin had a relaxed sort of authority, and Iskander found himself feeling at ease.

He searched the roof of the cockpit and found a miniature stick-figure diagram of a lift, complete with two arms and legs built of small indicator lights. All four of the limbs shone a cheerful emerald color.

"All green," he said.

"Good. Five thousand might have been money well spent."

Iskander grinned broadly for the first time that day.

"Looks like you've already got drive assist turned on – that's good, leave it on. Make sure they're both on every time you start your lift, too. That's very important."

"Yes, ma'am, I found that out last night," Iskander said.

"That sounds like a story I'd like to hear, but save it for later. Go ahead, start it up."

Iskander reached above his head and gave the MAIN START dial an enthusiastic twist. Behind him, the engine issued a short, restrained moan, then quieted. The dejected sound was familiar – it was the same as when the lift failed to start in Arnold's lift lot.

Iskander's throat tightened.

"Give it another try," Ruin said.

Iskander twisted the switch again, but the engine only made the same subdued, unhelpful sound before settling into silence.

Iskander kept his back straight in his seat and his gaze fixed ahead, out the windshield. His skin flushed, heat spreading down the back of his neck. There was a feeling in his chest like smoke from a hopeful cinder on damp kindling, abruptly crushed by a boot.

Ruin drummed her fingers on the lip of the cockpit's top hatch and hummed to herself.

"Well, you drove it here, so that's promising."

Despite the words, her tone implied more patience than optimism.

"It feels locked up!"

The shout came from outside, near the back of his lift, and had an excited lilt.

"That's Showe." Ruin sounded deeply relieved. "Come outside, and listen closely to what she says."

Ruin slid off the roof and Iskander followed her down the ladder.

They found Showe hanging off the back of Iskander's lift, clinging to small toeholds on the exterior of the engine. She was near Iskander's age and wore a jumpsuit like Ruin's, but where Ruin's jumpsuit was clean, if drably colored, Showe's was almost gleefully filthy. Her jumpsuit's knees looked particularly downtrodden – the fabric was little more than large, black splotches of ingrained grime. Her head was deep inside a crevice of Iskander's engine bay, but as Ruin and Iskander neared, she dropped from her perch to land with a thud of thick work boots.

"Is this your lift?" She addressed Iskander eagerly, and he nodded.

"Air-cooled is a batshit-crazy choice for an engine this size – I like it. And it's two-stroke! Never seen that on a 49. Why won't it start?"

Under the enthusiasm of her questioning, the heat began to drain from Iskander's face. Nearby, Ruin studied them without speaking.

"I'm not sure. " He shook his head. "I just bought it yesterday."

Showe seemed unfazed by this lack of expertise.

"Well, I could feel the starter kicking, so that's good, but the rest of the block felt like it was seized solid. You drove it in here?"

She gestured at the entrance to the mitt.

Iskander nodded again. "I drove it all the way from Attowa."

"In soft-step gear." Ruin contributed casually, while her hands flicked through a series of complex, silent gestures.

Showe's eyebrows crinkled with interest.

"Oh, so it's stuck in soft-step?"

Iskander cleared his throat and hesitated.

"No. Driver was, though," Ruin said wryly, while her hands moved through several more signals that Iskander belatedly recognized as sign language.

Showe blinked several times, regarding Iskander, then Ruin, and then Iskander again as a small smile began to tug at her lips.

"Could running in soft-step all that time lock the engine up like this?" Iskander asked, a flush rising in his cheeks.

"No," Showe said, her smile still lingering. "No, that wouldn't hurt anything."

She turned and clambered back up the engine, peering into crevices on the massive motor.

"It's not common for a lift to run one minute and then totally lock up the next. This isn't your average 49, though. Whoever built this thing either knew ten times what I know …"

Showe clambered higher on the engine, slipping and emitting a frightened yelp before regaining her footing.

"… or they knew jack shit."

A few moments passed in silence as Showe continued her inspection, high aloft the ground now, up near the lift's tall exhaust pipes. Ruin shifted her weight to another hip, at ease as she watched the situation unfold.

Showe's head popped out from the engine's silhouette to regard Iskander with interest.

"Has it done this before? Does it usually start right up?" she asked.

"It wouldn't start when I first found it on the lot." Iskander replied, being careful to tilt his face straight toward Showe as he spoke. "I was poking around at the controls, and then it sat for a while, and then it started right up."

Ruin signed next to him as he spoke, and Showe's eyes moved back and forth between Ruin's hands and Iskander's lips.

"You didn't change anything to make it start?" Showe asked.

"I don't think so. It sat for a while, and then it just started."

Showe let out a long, considering hum, then her head rocketed back down behind the bulk of Iskander's engine.

"This thing's got a *hell* of an engine heater on it," she called. "The elements are spread out and linked across the entire block – never seen anything like it! Coolant and fuel heaters, too."

Her head appeared again above the silhouette of the engine, regarding him with interest.

"So, what does that mean?" he asked.

"I've got no idea, but it's all custom. Even serious cold weather heaters just warm a part of the block, sometimes one of the reservoirs. This is more thorough. It looks …"

Showe paused, her expression contemplative and her face backlit by warm sunrays.

"… purposeful," she said at last. "And done by someone smart, who knew what they were doing."

She paused again.

"Probably."

She slid down across the bulk of the lift's engine block, landing on the pavement next to Iskander.

"Mind if I look inside the cab?" she asked, holding out her hand expectantly.

"Sure," Iskander said, placing the ignition badge into her outstretched hand. "But I thought it was called the cockpit?"

There was a pause while Ruin signed next to him, and when she finished, Showe let out an indelicate guffaw.

"It's a lift, not a spaceship." She pushed his shoulder teasingly. "What's your name?"

"Iskander."

"I'm Lashowe, and my callsign is Showstopper, so you can just call me Showe for both," she said. "Nice to meet you."

She sidled past him and up his lift's ladder, disappearing inside the cab's side door. A warm breeze sighed across the parking lot as Iskander and Ruin stood, the wind twitching the ragged hem of Iskander's coat where it hung from the crook of his arm. His stomach grumbled again.

"Showe's about as good as it gets for lift mechanics, but if she can't fix you up, do you need a ride home?"

"No, I'll just take a car," Iskander said, fully intent on instead using his bicycle, chained to a pole outside the mitt's entrance.

Ruin nodded absentmindedly and stared over Iskander's shoulder. He turned to follow her gaze across the parking lot and saw Paulette emerging from the hourly worker's office alongside a man Iskander did not recognize. They were distant, but Iskander saw that he wore a jumpsuit like Ruin and Showe, held a child's car seat in one hand, and walked close at Paulette's side.

The little boy who had been sleeping in Paulette's office was now squeezed between Paulette and the man, holding one of each of their hands as they walked three abreast.

"That's Preen, next to Paulette," Ruin commented. "He started here a bit like you, just showed up with a lift one day. Their little boy is Milo."

Her voice was warm.

"Don't let today fool you, Paulette's good people. It's just that after she married Preen, she started wanting safety at the mitt like you and I want air to breathe."

In the distance, Preen busied himself with the car seat while Paulette waved in their direction, then tickled Milo and pointed to them. Iskander and Ruin waved back while young Milo stood nonplussed throughout the exchange. The car seat now secured, Preen entered the car having never acknowledged them.

Another figure emerged from the hourly worker's door, a woman in a jumpsuit of soft, cornflower blue that contrasted the drab suits worn by Showe, Preen, and Ruin. She walked with long strides, closing the ground between herself and another vacant car before she spotted Ruin and waved. Ruin waved back.

"That's Cinder. Showe's sister. She drives biggest rig on the mitt, so you couldn't miss it even before she painted it orange."

The door to Iskander's cab banged open above them. Showe burst from the cab and swarmed down the lift's ladder at an alarming speed, rushing past them without speaking. Her eyes were wide and her smile was broad.

She clambered up the lift's broad engine, periodically stopping to press her hands against a pipe or blocky metal surface. Her smile grew wider, until finally she laughed aloud with such hearty delight that it tugged a smile from Iskander even as his eyebrows tightened in confusion.

"Are you kidding me?" she shouted at him from atop his engine, the exuberance in her voice taking any sting out of the question. "Are you *actually* kidding me?"

"Ah …"

"Where did you buy this thing?"

"Arnold's Lift Lot," he said, while Ruin signed.

"That scrapyard in Attowa? No *fucking* way. How much?"

"About five thousand."

Showe squealed with glee.

"Okay," she said. "I think I know what's going on. I'm not sure, but I think I know. I read about this, *once*, a really long fucking time ago."

She crawled at a distressingly careless speed from atop his engine and into his cab via the top hatch. A moment later, the engine gave a loud, split-second groan, stuttered, then roared to life. Belts spun and a brief puff of white smoke spouted from the tall exhaust pipes.

Iskander drank in the noise and felt an enormous, oily weight flee from his chest. Ruin gave him a congratulatory bump on the arm.

Showe catapulted out of the cab again, this time clutching her personal and sliding one-handed down the access ladder to alight next to them.

"I pulled the motor's multidata and proofed it off the specs for my shop's printer. Not even fucking *close*! I doubt there's a printer anywhere on Sargasso that could re-print this engine to spec."

She looked up from her personal, locking gazes with Iskander. Her eyes were huge and her face was flushed, contrasting with bright, white teeth as she grinned at him. He smiled back, impulsively, as she continued to talk.

"The clearances inside this block are orders of magnitude tighter than the factory standard – they're so finely fitted that when the engine is cold, it's completely locked up, like a clenched fist. At first glance, it seems like the motor is just fucked. Once it warms up, though, metal expands, and the parts can finally move."

Showe shook her head in awe.

"It *can't* start cold, that's where all the extra heaters come in. It needs to be fed warm oil and fluids, intravenously. Like it's alive."

Iskander did his best to seem impressed, but his own cheer came from the engine starting at all.

"So, there's nothing actually wrong with it? These are good things?" he asked.

Showe slapped him on the shoulder, hard.

"They're *really* good. They mean horsepower. A fuckload of it."

She eyed the lift.

"I can't tell you exactly how much without putting this thing on a dyno, but it's a lot. Plus it's a two stroke. I'd guess you could lift at one, maybe even two classes above the normal GLC for a Hershaw 49."

"That's Cinder's weight class." Ruin sounded startled.

Showe nodded, quick and emphatic.

"Yep. I think it might be an old SOCS lift."

Iskander recognized the acronym from his studies – SOCS stood for Superlow Orbit Catching Station. SOCS were the halfway point of a shipping container's journey to space, the platforms in the sky where the flying shipping containers landed before the last leg of their journey up enormously long tethers to true high-orbit shipping facilities.

Showe was still speaking.

"A couple decades ago the SOCS used lifts, just like the mitts down here use lifts, and they had to be super light because weight is a commodity up there. That would explain all the weird-ass ceramic parts in this thing – to cut weight. Plus it's super cold up there, so an air-cooled engine would be really efficient, and cut even more weight."

"Is there enough oxygen at that altitude to feed an engine?" Ruin asked, her hands flicking and gesturing in sign language.

"Maybe? That's why I said 'working theory'," Showe grinned. "But who cares? What I know for sure is there's a stupid amount of horsepower coming out of this motor. Your max GLC will actually be set by your super cap and your joint ratings, as weird as that sounds. If you were to run this thing in dual-supply, you'd probably tear the nips right out of their sockets."

Iskander tried not to look overwhelmed by the vocabulary. Ruin glanced at his face, then cut in.

"What does he need to know day-to-day, Showe? For maintenance and driving."

Showe blinked slowly, disappointed by their mutual failure to share her exhilaration.

"Not much. It won't start unless you hit the auxiliary heater button a few minutes beforehand. That activates all the heaters and pumps, it's set up to be dummy proof. Tank's pretty full, probably another few months before it'll need fuel. From the driver's seat it's a pretty normal lift, just weirdly powerful and light for a Model 49."

"But I can use it? I can work?" Iskander asked.

Showe's nose wrinkled as she regarded him, seeming perplexed by the question.

"Of course. It's obviously been neglected, but I've seen 49s go through a lot worse."

She eyed the lift wistfully.

"Maintenance on that motor is going to be on the high side of normal, though. You don't owe me anything, all I really did was look at it, but maybe you could bring it by my shop sometime? I can cut you a deal on a tune-up, and maybe just check it out for an hour or two, for my own curiosity?"

"He'll bring it by this week." Ruin spoke to Showe, but Iskander guessed that the hint of firmness in her tone was for him. He beamed a smile at both of them, still blissful at the noise of his lift's loping idle.

"I'll be there."

Ruin rapped her knuckles twice on the side of Iskander's lift.

"Okay, we're halfway through my lunch break, and I've still got to teach Iskander how to drive this thing without hurting himself. You're sure he's all set for now, Showe?"

Once Ruin finished signing, Showe nodded, then eyed his lift's spinning belts and shuddering exhaust pipes with longing.

"This week?" she asked again.

Iskander nodded firmly.

Ruin climbed his lift's ladder to her seat above the cab's top hatch, and Iskander climbed to the cab. Showe stepped back as his lift's engine revved and the machine rose from its parking stance, legs articulating to a fully upright stance. Iskander peered out the side window at Showe, and found her staring up at the cab. She gave him a small wave.

Ruin's voice was patient. "Iskander, you're in charge of 49 tons of swinging steel. Can you spare some attention for it?"

Iskander turned quickly from the window and nodded. "Yes, ma'am."

"Good. See the compass bubble on your dash? Use the degrees – the numbers inside the bubble – when you're giving other drivers directions, or receiving them. Just saying north, south, east, and west won't cut it when every square foot around you is piled with freight."

"How do I talk to the other drivers?"

"Your lift has loudspeakers. We'll deal with that later – for now, yaw to 150, then start walking. Slowly. Do you know how to yaw the cab?"

"Yes, ma'am."

Iskander tilted the control sticks and the cab swiveled, while the legs underneath remained stationary. The compass bubble on the dashboard spun lazily until the needle rested on 150.

"Enough with the ma'am, just 'Ruin' is fine. Press the throttle when you're ready – with drive assist on, the legs will take care of themselves no matter which direction the cab is facing."

Iskander pressed the accelerator pedal with his toe, and the lift walked forward with heavy, rhythmic thumps that bumped the cab up and down. Iskander saw he was aimed for a long strip of leafy trees that sheltered under the cargo thrower's elevated track, far away from the parking lot, the office building, and shipping containers.

"Once we're off the pavement, press that little switch on the left control stick, about halfway down."

Iskander waited for the rhythmic clacking of his lift's feet on pavement to turn to dull, earthy thumps that were more felt through the seat than heard. He pressed the switch and a horn outside blared zealously, a short but deafening report that shattered the emptiness of the parking lot and echoed from the distant office building and stacks of shipping containers. Over his head, Iskander heard a repetitive clicking noise, mechanical and faint but constant. He kept pressure on the foot pedal, and the lift continued walking at its measured pace.

"That horn sounds when you turn off soft-step gear, to let everyone know you'll be doing some fast moving," Ruin explained from up above. "Your hazard lights come on automatically, too. You might be able to hear them, kind of a clicking noise from up top. Go ahead and step on the throttle a bit."

Iskander pressed harder on the pedal and the lift lurched to a jog, the thuds of its footsteps coming faster. The engine hummed louder behind him, and up top, Ruin raised her voice to talk over it.

"The throttle won't acknowledge sudden changes, since you've got drive assist turned on. Even if you mash the throttle from a standstill, the lift will start with a walk and slowly build up speed."

She paused and took a breath, winded by her loud tone.

"Give it a little more throttle now."

Iskander stepped harder on the pedal and the lift burst into a powerful sprint, engine bellowing angrily, vibrations beating through the firewall at his back. The cab knocked to either side as the lift's feet landed hard, showering the nearby grass in clods of abused and uprooted turf. An excited grin split Iskander's face in half at the glut of noise and speed.

Above him, Ruin grabbed at the rim of the hatch, looking surprised and faintly alarmed. The trees were approaching fast in Iskander's windshield.

"Hard left!" she shouted.

Iskander swung the control sticks and the lift responded, body tilting to the side like a motorcycle leaning into a deep curve. The legs pumped up and down, maintaining speed, and Iskander felt the muscles in his stomach and back tighten to keep his body upright in the seat against the fast, deep lean. The trees were stripped from view as Iskander turned and the lift thundered down a bare dirt road that hugged the edge of the tree line. The road curved, and Iskander followed it with mild input on the control sticks.

Above him, Ruin had regained her composure.

"Keep on this road for about half a mile."

Iskander's lift sprinted past many small turnoff roads, each with signs declaring a sequence of letters and numbers.

"These are the freight yards for the different lifting classes. The lower the class, the lighter the weight. Cans get grouped at the catching pits and then piped up to these sites for handling."

Ruin was all but fully shouting over the roar of the engine and the rush of the wind.

"Hershaw 49s with factory nips like yours can lift up to class 3B, that's B as in butter. The 3 is the weight, the B is the nip dexterity required for the type of can."

A massive truck appeared on the road ahead, a squared black lump of a vehicle with a tiny, vestigial windshield, rumbling down the dirt road on muddy tires. It towed a long, tall trailer, a simple but massive rectangle of corrugated steel, several times the size of the pointed shipping containers. Iskander pushed on the control sticks, giving the truck ample space as his lift stomped past.

"What's nip dexterity?" Iskander raised his own voice over the clamor.

"Nip is short for manipulator – the things you use to pick up the cans. Oh, and a can is a shipping container. You've got the factory's B-class nips on there, forked-magnetic, good for most cans you'll come across at this mitt. You can go up to C-class if you've got the money, they can handle circular cans for liquid cargo and that'll open up a few more jobs, but anything beyond C-class is wasted on a freight lift. Showe's got F-class nips – five fingers and a thumb, with fully articulating wrists. She doesn't actually pick cans, though, she's emergency services. Her lift can dig people out of collapsed buildings without killing them, or do search-and-rescue where there's no roads, or in deep snow. They send for her from ten counties away when there's been a mining accident. Slow down!"

Iskander eased back on the throttle as they neared another turnoff road. The sign for this site had been vandalized with spray paint, but Iskander was able read "1A" under a face crudely sketched in neon yellow, with crossed eyes and a mouth that vomited brown and green streaks.

"Does 1A mean the lowest weight and dexterity class possible?"

"Gold star for you. Welcome to the slop pit."

PASSERBY AND storefronts slid past Iskander's windshield as his rented truck wound through the heart of Picochee: a grid town of low brown shops, houses, and clean-swept sidewalks that baked in the sun. The walkways and streets were paved with a dark, mottled stone quarried from local mines, and as the sun heated them, the pavers released a dusty, mellow smell.

The wind breezing into his cab's open windows was a luxury. A checkered cloth laced with pleasant herbal oils was tied around his face – Paulette had forced tiny bottles of scent into his hand with a stern but oddly pitying look on the third day of his work in freight zone 1A – the slop pit. The oils were a kind gesture but a frail defense against the pervasive, dense stink of the slop, and Iskander pulled the scented handkerchief from around his mouth and nose to gratefully breathe the fresh wind from his cab windows. He leaned back in the seat and let his eyes close as fatigue and the summer breeze washed over him.

Lifts were not permitted to walk within city limits, so instead, his lift squatted on a hired truck's flat bed, surrounded by a cage of steel beams as thick as tree trunks, all growing from the vehicle's frame.

A pothole jostled the truck's suspension and rocked Iskander upright in his seat. He opened his eyes resentfully, and saw passersby on the sidewalks exchanging startled looks as the truck rumbled past with his lift aboard, their noses wrinkling in distaste. The slop pit had left gloppy chunks of paste on his lift's legs and manipulators, and he knew the murky smell traveled. The rest of the lift's frame had a thinner coating of goop, aerosolized under his lift's heavy footsteps into a thin, slippery film that floated as high as his windshield. Iskander had spent the first day of work in the pit peering through glass gone blurred and streaky from the sprayed slop, his windshield wipers useless after the second or third pass, until Ruin left a bottle of acidic windshield washer fluid at the foot of his lift's stepladder.

General economics classes had taught Iskander that Sargasso was primarily an importer of overspace goods, so the slop pit was one of the few freight zones at the Picochee mitt to handle outgoing cargo. The oozing material was simply referred to as "slop," and no one had a convincing explanation for what exactly it was, or why it needed to be shipped overspace in such quantity – universally, other people had simply accepted that it was so, and avoided offering to help. As Iskander worked long hours in long days, breathing through a handkerchief where Paulette's delicate herbal oils wilted against the avalanche of fumes, he had tried hard to hold on to this glimmer of validation – somewhere, someone was waiting on him for their shipment of slop.

The truck hit another bump in the road that rattled Iskander's lift, shaking free several moist, gritty pounds of scum that slapped onto the sun-warmed steel of the truck bed. On the sidewalk outside Iskander's windshield, a startled father spun a stroller on its wheel, pointing the indolent child safely away from the truck. Iskander rolled his eyes.

After several more turns, the truck edged toward the outskirts of Picochee, eventually turning into a small, fenced parking lot. A handful of lifts crouched in parking spaces, and a warehouse-like structure with tall bay doors faced him from across the lot. Inside, lifts lay sprawled on the ground, one per bay, a few with limbs hung in the air by massive slings like broken-limbed patients recovering in greasy cement hospital beds.

A mechanical arm whirred to life above Iskander's lift, pulling on braided steel cables as thick as tree limbs that looped through eyes on his lift's frame. Iskander pressed his back into the cab seat as his crouched lift floated into the air, suspended by the cables a few inches above the truck's bed, and glided with slow, hydraulic smoothness out over the empty pavement of the parking lot. The steel arm overhead issued a loud clack and began to pay out cable, lowering Iskander's lift to the ground. A massive clamp unlatched with a bang, the fat steel cable zipped into a spool on the truck, Iskander's personal dinged an alert, and the fee for the trip was extracted from his account.

Iskander opened his cab door and the true stink of the slop hit his nostrils – heavy like wet sand, jarring like a slap in the face. He held his breath and climbed the ladder down from his cab as the flatbed truck, quiet despite its bulk, maneuvered itself out of the parking lot.

He wanted to hurry as he walked, to leave the cloud of stinking vapor before it soaked any deeper into him, but exhaustion was a stony weight in his boots.

"Iskander!"

He blinked slowly and saw Showe crossing the parking lot with bounding steps.

"You're here!"

"I'm here," he repeated, waiting until she was close enough to read his lips.

He hadn't seen Showe since she examined his lift, days ago in the parking lot at Picochee mitt, but her tone was warm and enthusiastic – a pleasant change from the sternly watchful Paulette and casually aloof Ruin. Her jumpsuit was, if anything, even filthier now than when he had last seen it, contrasting with a bright white undershirt peeking from under her collar.

"Lots of people *say* they'll come," Showe said. "I'll tell them, 'that part really needs to get looked at,' and they'll say, 'Yep, I'll bring it by.' And then they *don't*. And then the thing breaks. And *then* they come."

Iskander blinked tiredly and tried to focus. The pace of her speech felt torrential but was, he suspected, quite normal and friendly.

"Sounds silly of them," he said at last.

Showe nodded in emphatic agreement, then peered closer at him.

"Hey, you look like shit."

Her tone was unflinchingly affable, and Iskander laughed. She grinned at him, her small nose wrinkling.

"It's been a long week," he allowed. "But I got my license." He produced his personal and tapped to the certification, then showed her the screen.

Her jaw fell open.

"Isn't that, like, eighty hours?"

"Eighty-three." He said, and counted out 8 and 3 using his fingers.

Showe's eyebrows drew together in genuine concern and she issued a soft moan, as though Iskander was a baby that had just done something adorable.

"And now you're coming by my shop, too? Have you even gone home yet?"

Iskander shrugged.

"I promised I'd come." He said, and gestured at his lift. "And I want to make sure I'm all set for next week."

Showe puffed air through her lips.

"Your lift is fine, eighty-three hours in the slop pit is nothing for that motor."

She turned on her heel and motioned him to follow.

"Come inside. There's a back area where you can wait while I do some diagnostics. It's kind of a members-only place, but nobody is using it right now, and you've earned it after the week you just had. Just don't tell my other customers."

Iskander followed Showe past cavernous bay doors toward a small side entrance. He peered inside the bays as they walked – two other workers in greasy jumpsuits, all roughly the same age as him and Showe, crawled over lifts that lay supine on the cement floor. Showe called into one of the bays as they passed.

"Got a 49, just came from the slop pit! Hose it off and lay it out in bay nine!"

An acknowledging shout came from inside, and one of the workers rolled a large cart out of the bay doors and across the lot toward Iskander's lift. The cart's caster wheels clacked on the pavement, hoses and power washing nozzles jingling on its many hooks and pump housings as the man hustled it across the parking lot.

Showe opened the side entrance door ahead of him, revealing a small, sparsely furnished waiting area. The door snicked closed behind them, sealing in the quietness of the room's empty plastic chairs and automated reception desk – no customers waited despite the many lifts that lay in the bays outside.

"It's back here."

Showe stepped through a door marked Employees Only. The next room held several hugely puffy recliners, a wet bar, and tables with bowls of snacks scattered across them. Board games in varying stages of completion further complicated the tabletops, and massive display screens covered two of the walls. A stray plastic game piece rolled away from Iskander's foot.

"This is where me and some of my friends hang out. It's kind of a club. But you can be an honorary member for the day."

The cushions on the recliners looked so catastrophically plush that Iskander felt weak in the knees. He edged towards them.

"Are you sure? Your friends won't mind?" he kept his face squarely to hers, where she could see his lips.

Showe shook her head.

"It's my shop, not theirs."

Iskander noted that this was not quite what he had asked, but he was now more than halfway towards the nearest recliner. Showe motioned to the snacks strewn around the room, and to a small refrigerator.

"Help yourself. I'll be at least an hour with your lift."

Iskander settled gingerly into the recliner, trying hard to remain upright and attentive toward her, all the while suspecting he might be swaying with exhaustion. The recliner was slick and cool, and the stuffed cushions were pressed to the perfect firmness by countless hours of use. He blinked hard and forced his eyes to widen.

"Thanks. Really." Iskander said, then hesitantly made the hand sign for "thank you."

Showe smiled, and her nose wrinkled with the movement.

"I like to help sometimes, when I see help's needed," she replied. "That's a quote from Ruin. Sit tight, I'll be back in a bit."

As Showe left, she waved her hand over a light switch, cutting the light in the room to a dim glow. Iskander was asleep before she had finished closing the door.

ISKANDER STARTED awake at a sharp kick to his boot. His eyes pulled open stickily, like an old dog dragged from slumber by the arrival of a stranger in the house.

"This is a private room."

A man leaned over the recliner, pushing his face close to Iskander's. He was in his late twenties, with a shaved head and a sinewy build, wearing the top half of a jumpsuit bunched and tied around his waist. His eyes were big, and angry.

"Get the fuck out."

"Take it easy, he's probably a customer," said an unfamiliar woman's voice. Iskander saw a cornflower blue jumpsuit in the corner of his eye.

"Well, this is *our* space. Customers stay the hell out."

After he spoke, the man kicked Iskander's boot again.

"Preen!" The woman snapped. "This is *Showe's* shop, not yours. Cool it."

Iskander rubbed his eyes. His heart was beating fast, but his head felt stuffed with fog as the woman turned her gaze on him.

"Sir? Do you know you're in a private area?"

Her voice was patient but firm.

"You'll need you to wait out in the lobby," she continued. "This area isn't for customers."

Iskander cleared his throat and sat up.

"Showe said I could wait in here."

"She did?" The woman's voice was intrigued, and Iskander turned to face her.

She was regarding him with eyes inset under plucked, graceful eyebrows, and she bit into an apple with a crack that carried in the dim, quiet room. Preen had leaned back out of the warmth of Iskander's breath but remained standing above him, arms folded, mouth flat.

Iskander recognized the cornflower-blue jumpsuit now – the woman was Cinder, Showe's older sister. She splayed her body over her chair more than she sat in it, like a vine draping its surroundings in heavy, leafy shoots, displaying primal entitlement to everything nearby with a claim as effortless as it was absolute. If Showe was a windstorm in springtime, her sister was moonlight on a sweltering summer night.

"You must be Iskander."

"That new guy?" Preen spat.

Cinder cocked her head, studying Iskander. He endured the scrutiny passively, welcoming the opportunity to sit quietly. She completed her survey and made a soft, indistinct noise – perhaps surprised, or displeased, or intrigued, Iskander could not discern which.

"This is the fighter's room," Preen gruffed. "He hasn't earned the right to be here."

Cinder puffed air from her lips in obvious annoyance.

"This is a lounge in the back of a repair shop."

Her voice held an odd finality, and Preen only stood tall and eyed Iskander fiercely for another few moments before he backed away and opened a nearby refrigerator. He pulled a bottle out and settled into an empty armchair, pulling his personal from his jumpsuit and beginning to tap away at it as he drank.

"I know about the lift fights," Iskander said.

Cinder's eyes snapped to him, focusing without friendliness, only intensity. Preen chuckled and continued reading from his personal.

"No, you don't," she said, and took another bite of apple.

"Sure I do. I've watched them a few times on the feed, everyone has. And it's not hard to figure it out, around all those lifts at the mitt."

Preen guffawed again but the noise sounded forced, as though he did not find Iskander's statement to be actually laughable, but was at least invested in ensuring Iskander thought he did.

Cinder tapped her fingernails on the table several times, considering Iskander as she chewed a bite of apple.

"I heard you're new, but nice," she said at last. "So, please give me your undivided attention."

Iskander had already obeyed – her eyes were hard, bright stones holding him in place, vise-like, as she spoke.

"You want to talk about the fights, you do it elsewhere. Not in my sister's shop. Tracking?"

Iskander nodded.

"You should listen to her."

Ruin's weighty, accented voice surprised Iskander – he had not heard her enter. Cinder stood and left through the door to the waiting room, pausing to touch Ruin's forearm as she passed – a short, familiar squeeze passing between the two of them. As the door swung open, Iskander glimpsed Showe in the waiting area.

"She's just being careful, but you should take the lesson," Ruin said, turning again to Iskander and in doing so, effortlessly commanding his complete attention. "There's a couple drivers in Picochee County Correctional right now, with their lifts impounded."

"I've been in there," Preen interjected, seeming satisfied. "You'd get eaten alive."

Ruin eyed Preen flatly, but said nothing.

"Is that why people are cagey about the fights? They're illegal?" Iskander asked, speaking quietly and glancing at the door where Cinder had exited.

"Not exactly illegal, but definitely not good civic duty. It's a gray area. There are arrests sometimes, but no big crackdowns. The fanbase is big enough that anybody who *really* tried to shut it down would be voted out of office, but the betting money will bring the cops sniffing around, from time to time. And there's the weapons. The rules are pretty clear, but every once in a while someone builds something a little too scary, and we all have to tread lightly for a few months."

Showe and Cinder entered the room with a faint squeak of the door hinge.

"Ruin, I just got through being mean to him," Cinder said, her hands twisting as she signed alongside her speech. "No fight talk back here."

Ruin shrugged apologetically, her own fingers gesturing. "It's nothing he couldn't have found on the feed."

"You get two grand just for competing. Top fighters can take in fifty-large in a season," Preen announced proudly. His hands stayed immobile, and Iskander was abruptly, keenly aware that only he and this man were not accompanying their speech with sign language.

"They give you money just to compete?" Iskander asked.

"It's for repairs," Ruin clarified. "Funded by the adverts and betting tariffs, mostly, but they need to offer it otherwise no one could afford to play. Still, you can run up ten times that if things get hairy in a match."

Iskander considered his own lift, his lifeline to food and funds, almost two years of effort and savings crystallized into solid steel and rubber. He imagined it smashed and broken, and felt queasy.

"So, you all are ... fighters?"

Cinder and Showe said nothing, while Ruin held up her hands innocently.

"I just hear things," she said.

Speaking at nearly the same time as Ruin, Preen pounded his fist on the arm of his recliner. "Number two seed in the league, right here. I leave 'em bleeding."

Ruin cast Preen a disappointed look.

"Preen, you've got a kid. Be more careful."

Preen gave a small shrug that tried, and failed, to be aloof and dismissive.

"He's not a cop. Just look at him."

Everyone looked at Iskander.

"Not a cop," Iskander confirmed.

"Something a cop would say." Ruin's tone was parchingly dry, and her hand signs adopted a slow, sweeping quality that even Iskander could recognize as sarcastic.

Preen scratched at his neck, hard enough to make his fingernails flex from the pressure. A worried look passed across his face like a ripple in a tossed blanket, before it was masked by nonchalance tinged with pulsing aggression.

"Good thing you're not a cop, or I'd beat the piss out of you."

Iskander looked at Preen curiously, but didn't respond. Cinder and Showe looked on with quiet interest from behind a table littered with snacks and board game pieces. As he glanced at them, Showe caught Iskander's eye and grinned at him, making something tiny and warm wriggle briefly in his chest.

Ruin was motionless, aloof if not exactly oblivious. Her mood seemed to match that of the room in general – amused, or at least idly interested. Even Preen's harshness felt largely reflexive – after a sidelong glance at the women, the wiry man took another pull from the bottle and settled back into his seat, abruptly content to ignore them all.

No one, Iskander realized, was waiting for him to leave. He rolled the thought over in his mind, looking from all sides, checking carefully for dents and flaws and finding none.

It felt good.

He glanced again at Showe, and took a breath before speaking.

"So, how could someone new get started in the fights?"

"Easy there, cowboy." Ruin smiled. "First of all, you have to get invited. Second of all, there are two mandatory safety upgrades called a bathtub and a cover plate, and those aren't cheap. Plus a weapon of some kind. Really, you should have a whole spare junker lift, something that won't cost you too much if it gets trashed. Finally, I don't really like *anyone* getting involved in the fights, least of all green drivers. Focus on the basics for a few months. Make some new friends around the mitt. If you really want to fight, the right people will find you."

"His motor would be great for the fights."

It was the first time Showe had spoken, and her voice chimed cheerfully against the gravity of Ruin's tone.

Ruin gave Showe a dark look, and Preen activated as though a button on him had been pressed.

"What kind of motor?" he asked.

"It's a two-stroke with carbide internals. Air-cooled, although it's maybe more accurate to call it oil-cooled – the pan is twice the size that displacement should need, so the oil's definitely doing more than keeping the clutches wet. My best guess is that it's an old SOCS lift, but I'm still figuring it out."

Showe paused to give Iskander a substantial look.

"Just to be clear, I'm *not* saying you should join the fights right now. But you do have a hell of an engine, if you ever decide to."

"I'll invite you and give you a weapon." Preen's eyes were lively now. "Got some armor scraps, too. Real men don't have a spare lift, they fight with their daily driver – I do. And you *like* this little backroom club, don't you? I can see it."

Iskander started, and felt heat rise in his cheeks. Preen wasn't nearly as incurious as he appeared.

"You want to hang here, for real, you need to fight," Preen continued, his tone harsh. "You can even start this season – first bracket is next week."

Iskander opened his mouth to respond, but Showe spoke first.

"Preen, lay off the new guy or I'm going to tell your wife." Her voice became mockingly infantile. "Wouldn't want Paulette to come and give her baby a spanking, would we?"

Preen's mouth twisted, but to Iskander's surprise, he stayed silent.

"What's a bathtub?" he asked, keeping his voice steady.

"Heavy duty protection, embedded into the frame around the driver," Ruin said. "And the cover sheet is an armor plate that gets bolted over the windshield – it's studded with cameras and sensors so you can see through it. They're both required to compete."

"He'd be fine," Preen said dismissively, and directed his attention back to Iskander. "Plenty of folks run in drive assist the whole time. Just point and shoot."

"Aren't those parts expensive? Why would you give me a weapon for free?" Iskander asked.

"I upgraded to better stuff, so it's just taking up space in my shed. Plus, I'm a nice guy."

"Always free cheese in a mousetrap," Cinder contributed, to no one in particular.

"Shut up, Cin," Preen said.

Ruin turned, facing her entire profile to Iskander. He was still sitting in the recliner, and she seemed to tower above him.

"You get two thousand for competing, but even experienced, cautious fighters can leave the pit with twice that in repairs. Some fighters are respectful, and some are not. You can pop your mercy flag and they'll just keep attacking. Sometimes people lose their entire lift – it happened just last season."

Iskander thought he saw Showe's cheeks flush dark red, just as Ruin finished speaking and signing.

"Give it some time, build up some hours, not to mention some money," Ruin continued. "Then fight."

Before Iskander could respond, Preen interrupted.

"There were a bunch of murders in Pink Lake last night," he announced, his eyes fixed on his personal. "Jacked the bank and killed four dozen."

"Four dozen *people*?"

"Serves those rednecks right." Preen grinned.

"What the fuck is wrong with you?"

"How far away is Pink Lake?"

"Aren't you from a border town, too, Preen?"

All at once, a dinging, vibrating alert rang across the room from the pockets of Ruin, Showe, Preen, and Cinder. Everyone except Iskander.

Preen swiped and tapped at his personal, then sighed.

"Season is postponed. Must be the attack, they were going to hold one of the matches at Pink Lake."

"How long?"

"Until further notice. I'd guess at least a few months." Preen looked up from his personal to lock eyes with Iskander. "How long does it take you to grow a spine?"

ISKANDER SLID his papers across a brushed steel shelf scarred with swirls and scratches, until the pages edged under the glazed window. Behind the glass, Rico's heavy, hairy hand scooped up the sheaf and held it under a tall device on the desk, which emitted a loud beep.

"GLC?"

"Three," Iskander said.

"Nip dexterity?"

"B as in butter."

"How long?"

"All day, if you can."

A pause, and the muffled sound of fingertips tapping a personal's glass panel behind the window. A final resounding tap, and Iskander's personal dinged an alert.

"Head down to 3-Butter-7," Rico said. "Look for the Herschevits trucks. Sixty-two cans, should keep you busy."

Iskander said his thanks as the man slid his papers back through the window. The metal shelf was cool under his fingers.

* * * * * * * * * *

The sun was warm on Iskander's back as his teeth cut into an apple. A trickle of juice made its way down his chin, and he wiped his mouth with his jumpsuit sleeve before leaning back on one arm.

He sat a comfortable two stories in the air on the flat roof of his lift's cab. Other parked lifts were arrayed around him, engines ticking gently as they cooled while their drivers browsed at a handful of food trucks that had braved the mud of the loading lot and now waited, arrayed in a neat semicircle, awnings opened wide with steaming food jutting out under the noses of customers.

Two of the food trucks had real cooks laboring within, and those drew the longest lines, but most were automated. On the rare days when Iskander didn't pack his lunch at home, he ate from the driverless trucks. Their food was brown, hot, and uninspiring, cooked *en masse* by computerized ovens and fryers, but it was cheap and filling.

A few lift drivers had disappeared from the scene outright, taking cars outside the mitt in search of a better lunch than any food truck could provide. Showe, Ruin, and Cinder were among those who left for lunch, along with a small group of other drivers that Iskander had gleaned were also competitors in the lift fights. They were a clique within the larger freight yard workforce, not only lunching together but often arriving and leaving for work as a group. Iskander had also noticed several romantic entanglements in the group, whereas the rest of the mitt's workers seemed largely content to ignore one another.

"About to flub," Preen said. "That Scorp over there."

He was pointing at a lift out in the loading lot with bright orange paint, and Iskander recognized the frame as a Bowen-Hitachi Scorpion – noticeably smaller than the blocky Hershaw lifts most drivers at the mitt used.

Preen had yet to voice anything but casual disdain for Iskander, but had begun eating lunch nearby to Iskander's parking spot once or twice a week. Preen was the only lift fighter who seemed apart from the clique, and today he was parked closer than ever to Iskander. They both sat on their lift's roofs, parked right next to each other, with only the radius of their respective cabs and a few feet of warm summer breeze between them.

Privately, Iskander suspected that Preen did not have many friends.

"Here it comes," Preen said.

The sound of a roaring engine reached Iskander's ears from across the loading lot. The small orange Scorpion was involuntarily leaning forward, legs splayed and braced for support under the shipping container in its forked manipulators, engine bellowing out every ounce of horsepower it had to give. A moment later, the lean deepened, the lift teetered forward, and the shipping container bumped unexcitingly to the ground. A collective jeer went up from the lift drivers in line for lunch.

"Flub!" The crowd shouted.

"Flub!" Preen shouted.

"Flub," Iskander said, quietly.

Trees and grass all around the space whistled in the breeze, and the air smelled green and warm.

"Dumb fuck." Preen settled backward into the roof of his lift's cab. "A Scorp is too small to be slinging cans."

Iskander pulled his personal from his pocket. Not for the first time, he blessed Paulette's purchase of an over-air antenna powerful enough to beat back Sargasso's constant soak of atmospheric interference, bringing any lift driver within 75 meters of her office the bliss of wireless connectivity that other worlds took for granted. He tapped on his personal's screen to bring up the accident report, generated automatically by the shipping container and doubtless forwarded to an insurance broker only a moment or two after the incident.

"Break something big?" Preen asked.

Iskander tapped a few more times on his personal and shook his head. "Just balloons. 63,000 of them. The container is scrapped but the balloons are fine. 94% salvageable."

"The fuck are they bringing in that many balloons for?"

"People got birthdays," Iskander said.

Preen snuffed dismissively.

Lunchtime was nearly over and a car appeared from the mitt's access road, slowing to a stop and emptying Showe, Cinder, Ruin, and a gaggle of other drivers onto the lot's gravelly mud expanse. Showe raised her hand and gave Iskander an energetic wave, then whipped something shiny up at him. Iskander's lift sat him two stories high, but her throw was strong and the sandwich smacked into his stomach, coming to rest in his lap.

A man Iskander did not know appeared at Showe's side, and a needle of disappointment arrowed through him as Showe grabbed the man's hand and began to talk animatedly. Iskander waved his thanks for the thrown sandwich, but her back was already turned.

* * * * * * * * * *

"I really don't like being lied to, Izzy."

Paulette's eyes were flinty, contrasting with the elegant warmth of her office's decor. Her and Preen's toddler, Milo, was nowhere to be seen, although his cot had the same untidy pile of blankets mounded on top.

"Ma'am?"

"Your background check finally came in. You were raised at the UU house in Picochee, twenty minutes from here."

Iskander swallowed, and within moments his armpits were damp with sweat.

"I ... yes, but I don't think I lied about that, ma'am. You just never asked."

"I asked about your family, and you said they weren't local. That was a lie."

"Oh. Oh, yeah." Iskander heard himself stammering, and could not stop. "I'm ... I'm sorry."

Several long moments passed as Paulette fixed him with a stare, her mouth drawn into a flat line.

"Can I still work here?" he asked at last, hating how small his voice sounded.

All the steeliness left Paulette's gaze at once, replaced by astonishment.

"You think I'm firing you? For fibbing about your family?"

"No, for ..." Iskander let the words die, realizing the thought had not yet occurred to her. A long moment passed, and when Paulette spoke again, her tone was wondering.

"... because of UU?" she asked.

Iskander felt his cheeks burning.

"Have people fired you for that, Izzy?"

He said nothing and Paulette's face did something strange, hardening and softening at the same time.

"If I fire you, it will be because you have failed so badly, or so frequently, that I decide your employment causes more harm to the mitt than your termination. No other reason. Perform, and don't start trouble, and you will be welcome here for as long as there are jobs in the morning queue. Understood?"

Relief cooled the flush from his skin, and he met her gaze.

"Yes, ma'am."

"I've told you not to call me ma'am, Izzy."

"Sorry ... Paulette."

* * * * * * * * * *

"C as in cat."

Behind the window, Rico tapped a few commands onto the screen before him, then peered at Iskander.

"Got yourself some C-class nips, eh?"

Iskander nodded, a little proudly.

"Just mounted last night."

"Good for you, coming up in the trade."

Rico punched a final command into the screen.

"Got quite a few C-class jobs today – lucky you. Want a slow and steady job, or a fast and spooky job?"

Iskander pondered.

"What's spooky about it?"

Rico tapped a few times on the screen.

"This one's Category N, that's 'Fireworks, Explosives, and Miscellaneous Volatiles.' Five cans in 45 minutes. That's all I can see."

"Who's the shipper?"

"RTG."

Iskander tapped his fingers on the metal shelf. RTG Express was one of the better shipping outfits – their cans were usually well-balanced.

"All right." Iskander felt a tingle of excitement. "Hit me with the fast and spooky."

Rico chuckled.

"You got it. 3-Cat-5-Xray. Like I said, five cans. And the RTG truck is due in an hour and fifteen."

Iskander's eyebrows narrowed.

"5-Xray? Where's that?"

"Just keep hauling down the main stretch, they keep Category N containers at the edge of the mitt. You'll see it."

Iskander's personal dinged an alert as the job was delivered to his queue.

"You want another job for after that?" Rico asked.

Iskander tapped at his personal, his eyes widening at the lavish wage for the job.

"Not with this kind of pay. I'll just do this and head home."

Iskander said his thanks as Rico slid his papers back through the window.

* * * * * * * * * *

Cinder and Ruin leaned on each other, bracing for support as their laughter saturated the air with gaiety. Iskander stood nearby as Showe picked her way around the black, sooty remains of his new C-class manipulators. Shards from his lift's lacerated, flaking windshield crunched between her boots and the concrete floor of her shop, and a gusty winter wind blew in through the open bay door.

Showe was using a small crowbar to probe the shredded metal and wiring that erupted from his lift's manipulator sockets. She made an indistinct noise that sounded like "oof" and gave one of the sockets an exploratory smack with the crowbar. A small hulk of twisted steel promptly fell free, smashing to the ground with a jarring clatter that made Showe shrink away. This elicited a fresh chorus of belly laughs from Cinder and Ruin.

Behind Iskander, Paulette appeared in the bay doorway, taking in the twisted remains of his C-class manipulators and the burnt streaks that slashed across the lift's cab and windshield like sooty flower petals. Preen's head appeared from around the bay door as well – he sneered briefly at Iskander's lift, then retreated.

Paulette patted Iskander's shoulder, smooth and shiny fingernails glinting colorfully, even as a string of giggles began to leak out of her.

"Volatile cargo?" she asked.

Iskander tried to smile ruefully, but only partway succeeded, and Paulette made an unhappy noise and wrapped him in a hug, standing high on her toes to reach over his shoulders. Iskander squeezed her in return and turned back to survey the damage, his gaze heavy.

Showe tapped a few commands into her personal and gave him a cheerful smile as two automated carts appeared, their caster wheels clacking as they rolled, each cart supporting one of Iskander's old B-class manipulators and a handful of other spare parts. Ruin and Cinder giggled one last time, a quiet laugh shared just between them, before Ruin tugged at Cinder's arm and murmured something coaxing. Cinder rolled her eyes but they approached Showe's repair carts together, tugging up their sleeves as they went.

ISKANDER SLID his papers across the brushed steel tray, scarred with swirls and scratches, edging his paper's corners under the glazed window. Behind the glass, Rico's hairy hand scooped up the sheaf and presented it to the device on his desk, which emitted a loud beep.

"GLC?" Rico asked.

"Three," Iskander said.

"Nip dexterity?"

"B as in butter," Iskander said, trying not to sigh.

"How long you want?"

"All day and then some, if you can."

Iskander's personal dinged an alert as the jobs arrived in his queue.

"Head down to 3-Butter-2 to get started. Stay warm out there."

Rico slid Iskander's papers back through the window and onto the metal shelf. Iskander began to turn on his heel, but Rico spoke again.

"Stop by the hourly office before you head down. She wants to talk to you."

Iskander did not bother zipping his coat for the short trip between the day worker's waiting room and Paulette's office, instead hugging it close to his body as he pushed through the door into the wind outside. Other lift drivers waiting in line grumbled at the hard and frosty torrents of air that shoved into the waiting room as he exited. He walked to the door of Paulette's office, slipping into the clean warmth inside and closing the door with a quiet, sealing snick.

Paulette's almond-shaped eyes studied him. Delicate jewelry dangled from her wrists – small, short chains resting on neat paperwork.

"How long have you been working at Picochee, Izzy?"

"About six months, ma'am."

"How many accidents?"

"Three, ma'am."

"Any flubs?"

"No, ma'am. Well, there was the accident recently. That can sort of exploded before it touched the deck, though, so I don't think it counts as a flub. Technically."

She smiled, and her teeth were very white.

"I've told you before, don't need to call me ma'am, Izzy."

"Sorry ... Paulette."

"Are you nervous?"

"I think so. But I guess I'm waiting to see why you called me here."

Paulette tapped a pen on her desk a few times before she spoke.

"You're not in here to talk about your accident. If people didn't have accidents with volatile cargo, those jobs wouldn't pay so much. But you kept yourself safe, and you kept everyone around you safe. As far as I'm concerned, you're square with me. Once you pay the negligence deductible, that is."

She reached into her desk and pulled out a small plastic badge, which she pressed against the tablet before her. The device beeped softly.

"You're in here to talk about this – it's an hourly laborer's permit. I'd like you formally join Picochee mitt's loading team. No more scrounging for jobs at the day work office – just come in, work your time, and leave."

"After I almost flubbed that can?"

Paulette nodded calmly, and Iskander studied the badge in her hand.

"Well, I don't mean to be rude, and I'm not saying no, but can I ask a few questions?"

She nodded.

"That waiting room I just came from is full of people who would love to get a badge. Some of them must have good records. Why not them?"

"How do you know they have good records?" Paulette asked.

Iskander hummed thoughtfully for a minute.

"I guess I don't. But there's thirty people in that room some mornings – at least some of them must be clean drivers, right?"

"Some of them," Paulette allowed. "But not many as clean as you."

She paused and seemed to consider her words.

"Driving a lift draws a particular sort of crowd. There's a certain grandness to it – big machines, big engines, carrying big stuff that's going big places. You'll see a lot of drivers getting their rigs custom paintjobs, comparing cans-per-hour, talking trash. They forget, I think, that they're at work. Then we get damaged freight, or missed shipments. Basically, bad business."

Iskander nodded quickly, keen to show his comprehension.

"Now, freight losses at *this* mitt are less than half the national average, and that's because I fired about twenty drivers the day after I took ownership."

Iskander's eyebrows climbed before he could control them, and Paulette allowed a rueful nod of her head.

"Sargasso is still frontier enough for freight lifts to be profitable, but only just. I take no pleasure in firing people, but either we stay competitive, or the shippers go a few counties over to an automated mitt, and then we're *all* out of a job. So, I cut folks who can't keep up, and reward folks who can."

Iskander could feel that his eyebrows were still pinched in confusion.

"And you want *me* to join that crew?"

Paulette nodded.

"I do. I think you see this job for what it is – a job. You're serious about it. You're carrying other people's things, expensive things, and you act like it."

She paused and tapped a finger against her lips.

"I was told once that you can find the best driver on the lot by finding the driver who never shows any skill at all. A driver who never puts themselves in situations where they *need* skill – that's a true expert. Those are the drivers who make good time, and don't crack cans by accident, which means they make money for the mitt."

She gestured to the tablet.

"You might not be that driver yet, but when I look at your steps-per-hour, cans-per-hour, accident rates, all your stats, really – I see a good foundation."

Iskander nodded as a warm flush tingled over his skin, accompanied by a sudden and embarrassing tightness in his throat.

It was just a job, he told himself firmly. Paulette was just a boss, offering a promotion. It happened every day, probably thousands of times a day, to thousands of workers standing across from thousands of bosses.

The humiliating lump in his throat remained, because even when he had done his best, and tried his hardest, it had happened every day to thousands of other people, and never to him.

"Well, thank you, ma'am. I mean, Paulette," he said as calmly as he could.

She gave a short, cool nod. "So, you'll take it?"

"Yes, ma'am."

"Don't you want to know the pay?"

Iskander hesitated. He would have accepted a pay cut, rather than a raise, if it meant she gave him that badge.

"Sure," he said, doing his best to sound casual.

"A thousand a week."

Iskander was struck by the feeling that if he were a cartoon, his eyes would have quadrupled in size as he danced with cottony sacks of cash clutched in each fist.

"Works for me," he said brightly.

"I'm glad. Here's your badge," she handed him the small disc of plastic. "It's symbolic, mostly, but you need to keep it in your lift at all times."

She was tapping away at her screen.

"You'll get a block of jobs delivered to your personal every Sunday. 50 hours' worth. If you need help or want to take time off, you still need to work your block, so you'll need to sell the time to one of the day workers, or ask one of the hourly workers to cover for you."

"Who's on the hourly team?"

"You already know Ruin, Cinder, and Preen. Showe is technically hourly, too, but she's mostly maintenance. There're a few others – you'll meet them."

"Preen is hourly?" Iskander heard the surprise in his voice, then stuttered as the wedding ring on Paulette's finger seemed to glint angrily.

"I—"

Paulette was fixing him with a very level look.

"—was just …" Iskander swallowed, "… he doesn't seem like he fits the profile you just described. About never showing flashy skill."

Paulette softened and gave Iskander a wry smile.

"You're not wrong. He's always worked fast enough to be profitable, but when Ruin first dragged him in here, there were months where he'd owe a third of his salary in negligence deductibles. One day I mentioned that I don't date men who leave cans cracked open in my yard, and a year later his stats were better than Ruin's and we were expecting little Milo."

She tapped her finger on her desk, watching him.

"But enough about that – there's a good living to be made here, Izzy. Stay careful, stay helpful, and I'll make sure you're well compensated. Does that work for you?"

He nodded, and she held out her hand for him to shake.

"Welcome aboard."

2 months before

EVA WAS warm. The blankets heaped on her were simple mats of pressed fiber, speckled with grassy straw. She suspected they were sheets of freight padding, not blankets, but they were improbably cozy when piled thick.

Sodden, icy air bathed her face in the dim morning. Nights had turned bitterly cold at Camp Albatross, while mornings were somewhat less cold but compensated with frosty dampness, and she was sleeping in a grassy field on a bare cot. This would have been cause for concern before Eva came to Camp Albatross, but now, both the blankets and the metal cot that separated her from the grass were luxuries that she did not take for granted.

In fact, metal cots on frosted grass offered the best night's sleep Eva had seen in days, despite the malicious and purposeful placement of the cots within mere feet of the dry, temperature-controlled interior of the barracks.

She had been at Camp Albatross for a month and was beginning to feel like a genuine soldier. She could hit a D-zone target with a rifle at 200 meters, she now had a favorite flavor of canned beans, and soldiery nicknames were flowing fast and thick within her fireteam – her own surname had been shortened from Sweetwater to Sweet, while Sandersenbach became Sandy and Urobuchi became Uro.

Less than a week ago, she had completed deep-insertion survival and extraction (DISE) training in the rainy mountains of nearby Maurit prefecture. She, Weiss, Sandy, Uro, and Talk were now designated Fireteam Marko – referential to their presumed fireteam leader, Chief Marko – and they had been dropped on an unmarked, craggy mountaintop with a terse directive to find their way back to Camp Albatross. The elevation had been breathtaking in both the metaphoric and literal senses – the vistas were beautiful and the altitude made it hard to breathe. The rocky terrain and gaspingly sparse oxygen might have been bearable on their own, had it not been for fifty-three hours of continuous rain.

Her socks were soaked through within hours. She had yanked on her boot laces with hands gone numb and slippery in the endless downpour, tightening them to keep even more water from intruding, but her efforts were only rewarded by a gush of water around her calves as the socks inside were squeezed like a full sponge.

They had been issued rain gear – stout, rubbery clothing in military hues – but there was no such thing as "waterproof" under the sluicing deluge and the constant motion of hiking. By the end of the first day, her clothes were saturated all the way to her undergarments. Her backpack was sodden, and its contents were only slightly less wet. Her sleeping bag, tied to the underside of her pack, was heavy and sopping as she crawled inside it, and became even more so as she lay it on the muddy ground. She had torn open a meal kit and found the food inside was soaked through, the chemical heater waterlogged and inert.

More than twelve hours of marching, of screaming to be heard over soggy mountain wind that pounded on their rubbery hoods, of slipping on mud and banging herself on rocky slopes, of gasping for whatever scraps of oxygen her lungs could claw from the air – through all of it, the thought of dinner had sustained her. Calories warmed by the chemical heater, chewed slowly, while her tortured muscles finally lay still.

She had not cried since that first night with Weiss and Uro, weeks ago, but as her flashlight glinted on a soupy brown slush that had once been a slice of cinnamon bread, she sobbed, and the tears did not make the inside of her sleeping bag any wetter.

By comparison, a metal cot on the grass plus a pile of warm blankets was on par with a metropolitan hotel. Furthermore, she was confident that the next stages of training would be straightforward because their drill instructor, Motty, had reappeared after abandoning them on the mountaintop at the start of DISE. Eva still hated Motty, of course, but DISE had taught her that the presence of a supervisor – any supervisor – likely indicated tolerable conditions ahead. Supervisors hated being trapped in the wind and rain as much as anyone else, and typically had warm, dry beds somewhere nearby. This meant their cruelty would reliably expire after only eight to twelve hours, whereas DISE had lasted more than a week, and so for all Motty's screaming Eva was happy to see him.

DISE had taught her that she could endure almost anything for eight to twelve hours, and so could Weiss, Uro, Talk, and Sandy. She had thought such fortitude belonged only to history's strongest, hairiest warriors, whereas Eva herself had once injured her lower back via a particularly enthusiastic sneeze. Her newfound and nearly bottomless capacity to endure, she suspected, was a gift given to any human who struggled alongside a group of close-knit compatriots, a common ability grown in the womb alongside ordinary tendons and unremarkable bones.

Eva tugged on the rough blankets to pull them closer to her face, her hands wrapped in fingerless gloves made of heavy knit fabric. Her hat was made from the same cloth and similarly colored, a drab green, and it shielded her head from the icy expanse of her pillow, which chilled the skin of her cheek whenever she turned her face against it.

Motty's boots thumped outside the door to the barracks nearby, and Eva sighed but kept her eyes closed, waiting. Finally, in the cold, misty air above the grass, Motty's whistle shattered the stillness with a warbling shriek.

Eva sat up and let the blankets fall from her shoulders as the sodden morning air oozed over her. She slept fully dressed in a drab green uniform, save for the black socks that poked out from the thick lining of her pants. She untied her boots, which hung by their laces from a frost-rimmed strut of her cot to keep them off the wet ground, and stuffed her feet inside.

She curled one arm around her wadded blankets, then kicked a lever on the cot that made it fold up in a clanging, spring-loaded movement. She lifted the collapsed bedframe with her free arm and marched alongside the rest of Fireteam Marko into the empty barracks nearby, where they placed the collapsed cots in neat rows along the wall and made tidy piles of their blankets.

Bedding put away, they lined up for inspection without speaking. Weiss faced her across the empty barracks floor, Uro and Talk locked eyes to her right, and Sandy stood alone on the end, facing an empty wall. Motty paced up and down the floor between them, eying their cots and blankets darkly but voicing no complaints. He blew another sharp note on the whistle, and they filed out of the barracks in silence.

The ground was warming under the morning sun, turning the frost into a chilly dew that coated Eva's boots as she trudged through the grass to the nearby road. Motty kept pace, a few feet behind their group.

A boat was upturned on the roadway, a hulking slope of gray steel like an immense but legless beetle. Another short blast from Motty's whistle, and they surrounded the boat, backs straight. The whistle shrieked again, and they knelt as one, lifting the boat to their shoulders. In fingerless gloves, Eva's fingertips numbed the moment they touched the icy metal. She rested the hull on her shoulder so her bare digits could splay away from the freezing steel.

The group waited with the heavy boat on their shoulders. Eva stood tall, not minding the weight as she once had, as seconds turned to minutes. Motty paced slowly around the group as the time stretched, watching.

Uro stood in front of Eva, and as the minutes ticked by, Eva saw her back begin to tremble. Uro was one of the toughest in the group, but she had taken a sickening plunge during rappel exercises the previous day, and was still far from healed.

Finally, Motty's whistle screeched again and they walked.

The road was smooth dirt, snaking through a handful of scattered buildings on the close-cut grass, mostly squat, two-story cubes and a few long, low barracks. Camp Albatross's mess hall was a lonely spot of color, yellow on the outside with a low red door. In the distance, another small group in green uniforms was running laps, and the quavering notes of their supervisor's whistle floated in the misty morning air.

Fireteam Marko trudged at a purposeful pace, leaving the buildings behind and entering the wooded paths surrounding Camp Albatross. The roadway roughened, dipping down and around hillocks and ruts in the terrain, occasionally producing a small runnel or hole in the roadway that they crossed with slow, careful steps. Eva's breath began to puff in white clouds in front of her, and the weight of the boat on her shoulder became unpleasant. In front of her, Uro drew in a ragged breath.

The path stretched on through the woods, winding downward now. The morning sun rose higher, and though the air was still cool, Eva felt the first hint of sweat on her neck under the thick, rough cloth of her cold weather uniform.

As they descended, the dark blue rim of a pond peeked at them from just under the heavy green boughs laced tightly overtop the forested path. Beneath their feet, the ground began to soften with moisture, and the heavy, tangy, organic odor of a wetland filled Eva's nose.

Sandy cursed softly as they heard the first squelch underfoot, and Motty's baton hissed as he drew it. Sandy snapped his teeth together with a click as the path deteriorated from hard dirt to damp, glistening mud.

The water was close, but each footstep sank deeper than the last. The pond was overflowing, dirty and turgid with water that spilled flaccid rivulets into the trees around it. The muck sucked at their boots, Uro stumbled, and Eva winced under the sharp increase in the weight of the boat. She straightened her legs and pressed her palm low and firm against Uro's back. Uro panted for a moment, then straightened, lightening the immense weight of the steel hull on Eva's shoulder, and she patted the other woman's back reassuringly.

With heavy breaths and slow steps, they crept through the mud to the water's edge. A final blast from Motty's whistle and they dropped the boat the ground, flipping it over and readying it at the shoreline with practiced, wordless coordination.

"Push-ups."

Motty spat the word as he dangled the baton from its short leather strap, rocking it back and forth.

Eva knelt and braced herself in the push-up position – each of her comrades did the same, a neat line of angled bodies waiting for the next command. The mud stank of decay and glistened under her nose, and freezing sludge oozed between her fingers as her hands sank deep into the muck. Her gloves soaked through in moments, warm palms turning wet and icy. Eva closed her eyes and waited.

"Twenty!" Motty shouted, and his whistle screamed its frantic, piercing warble.

Up and down, the group's backs rose and fell. Push-ups came easily to Eva now, even weary as she was from the boat's weight, and she was quick to finish her count of twenty. She held herself up off the mud when the count was finished, and listened to her stomach grumble.

"Twenty!" Motty shouted again, with another blast from the whistle.

Eva completed her second set, but when she rested above the mud, her elbows trembled from the effort. A moment passed and Eva realized that Uro was lagging far behind, struggling to complete her twenty repetitions. Long seconds passed as her arms slowly bent up and down, and Eva heard her draw sharp, frantic breaths.

"Twenty!"

Eva squeezed her eyes shut and bent her elbows. Her arms shook, and a strangled gasp from Uro made her wince.

"Squats!"

The group got to their feet.

"One hundred!"

The whistle screeched and they began the exercise, feet squelching in the mud under their shifting weight. Uro's face was lined with pain and she only made it to eighty-three squats before kneeling in the mud, clutching her side, breaths whistling in and out in a ghastly cadence. Motty strode toward them, boots squishing in the mud, and stood over Uro. He addressed them as a group with his trademark disgust.

"Fireteam Marko, who is the weakest among you?"

Motty watched Uro grimly as he spoke.

"Recruit Urobuchi is weakest, Motty." Eva spoke in unison with the group.

"Who made her so weak?"

"We did, Motty."

Motty planted himself in front of Sandy, baton dangling from his thick wrist.

"Recruit Sandersenbach, why is Recruit Urobuchi so weak?"

"Because I—"

The baton jabbed into Sandy's stomach, jerking a ragged cough from him.

"—because *we* failed to secure the rope as instructed during rappelling drills, Motty. And as Team Leader, I was doubly responsible," Sandy finished.

"Correct!" Motty screamed the word.

Motty paced in front of the standing recruits, his grim tone and visage undermined by the extravagant squelch that accompanied each muddy step. Uro still sat in the mud nearby, panting.

"I don't like that, recruits – don't like it one bit. This time you failed to secure a rope, but do you know what happens when you ..." Motty paused to shoot Sandy a disgusted look, "... fail to secure a weapon?"

The group was silent, having long since grasped that unless Motty directed a question at one of them by name, he was most likely going to shout the answer himself.

"People get killed, that's what happens!" Motty yelled, spinning to face them. "Specifically, one of *you* gets killed. Then, I've got a dead recruit on my record. Then I lose sleep."

Motty began his slow, squishing march again.

"And I love sleep. Matter of fact, one thing gets me out of bed in the morning, and that's *faith*. Faith that in sixteen hours, I'll be able to get back in. *That's* how much I love sleep. So ..."

Motty paused in front of Talk, and leaned in close.

"... do you want me to lose sleep?"

This was tricky – Motty was inches from Talk's face, speaking to him directly, but he had *not* addressed Talk by name. A moment passed where Talk seemed to be weighing his options, before he finally replied.

"I—"

"—God damn it, Recruit Talk, I don't care what you want! I will personally ensure that you shitsacks do not make me lose one *wink* of sleep!"

Talk closed his mouth without speaking, and Motty nodded approvingly.

"Now, breakfast is in bags, floating out there."

Motty flung his hand out to cover the expanse of the pond.

"Thank you all for carrying my boat, I will gladly use it to survey your efforts. Prepare to get wet, troop. Clothes stay on, this isn't a nude beach."

Eva lined up with the others at the murky border of the pond, treading down the rough marsh grass, one foot on slick mud and the other in a puddle. The pond smelled distinctly like urine – it was not a large body of water, and was used daily by several dozen Camp Albatross recruits.

Talk leaned down to help Uro to her feet.

"Not necessary, Recruit Talk," Motty barked. "Recruit Urobuchi will wait on the shoreline. The first bag of breakfast will come straight back here to her."

Eva leaned forward and peered morosely into the inky pond. As she did, the loose bank of mud and marsh grass collapsed under one foot, and she nearly lost her balance before a hand gripped her elbow, steadying her. She turned to find Talk, standing close. Even through the fabric of her uniform, her skin felt warm under his palm.

She nodded thanks, and he nodded back. As Eva turned to face the pond, a smile that felt irrepressibly stupid tried to tug at her cheeks, and she forced her lips into a flat line. Talk straightened next to her, falling into line with the group, and she was keenly aware of the rise and fall of his shoulders as he breathed.

Motty walked with mud-sucked footsteps to the steel boat and busied himself getting it in the water, while their group stood in a neat line and waited for his whistle. After he was sure Motty was out of earshot, Sandy spoke quietly.

"Hey, guess my favorite swimming style."

No one replied, but after a month together, there was a sense of inevitability in the air as Sandy's eyes danced from one face to another.

"Guess. You have to guess," Sandy repeated.

"Breaststroke," Eva said at last, with a small sigh.

Sandy's eyes were wide with happiness, and he allowed a long pause before he answered.

"Yeah."

"I would have guessed dick stroke." Weiss's voice was droll.

From behind them, a chortle escaped Uro, but the noise quickly mixed with a pained gasp.

Motty's whistle shattered the air, and Eva was first to dive for the water. The pond was black and icy, and she held her breath as the cold attacked her skin. A shock lanced through the water as Talk landed next to her, and Weiss and Sandy soon after. The impacts were close, and Eva felt comforted by the shuddering rushes of noise and pressure that signaled her squadmates were close by.

She surfaced, gasped in a breath of frigid air, and glanced back at the shoreline as she began her swim. Motty had the boat in the water and Uro was leaning back in the mud, watching them swim with a look of odd contentment. Eva smiled as icy water sluiced across her cheek. She spotted a puffy plastic bag ahead of her, filled with rations, and threw her hand out. Digging deep into the water, she propelled herself forward with her squadmates close behind.

36 days before

WEISS LAY against a slope of black, crumbly dirt as she peered at the papery expansion screen of a militarized personal. She wore a suit of skeletal steel struts and drab camouflage cloth, sturdy technological scaffolding that cradled her from head to toe. A small tag on the bicep strut read `Enhanced Mobility Platform - Ruggedized, Mark 7`. Chief Marko simply called them battle jackets.

Weiss poked at the helmet that had fallen forward across her eyes, lifting it higher on her brow with a hand gauntleted in the battle jacket's steely armor. Soot group demanded that women's hair be gathered in a "tidy and inconspicuous" bun low on the back of the head. As a result, Eva, Weiss, and Uro's low-riding buns constantly tipped their helmets forward over their eyes, making it difficult to aim a rifle, which soot group seemed to accept as a necessary drawback to keep female hair tidy and inconspicuous.

Eva and Weiss lay on the sloping wall of a trench dug into a hilltop. The sightlines were excellent – if she poked her head up, she could see several miles of grass-carpeted terrain broken only by scrubby bushes and small stands of trees. On the opposite side of the trench, the scene shifted with jarring decisiveness from open prairie to an oddly squalid modernity – a built-up town where the buildings shared a blocky utilitarian aesthetic, built tall rather than wide and all showing the grayed, streaky patina of long neglect on their walls.

The architectural style, or lack thereof, was characteristic of Rugeran state-sponsored construction, and Eva assumed the buildings had once housed workers and families supporting some resource found in the empty fields and hills around them. Now, however, the town's narrow walkways were silent and the streets were empty – automated cars would not trawl the streets without passengers to serve.

"Unknown time to touchdown for command," Weiss said. "Fireteam Marko continues holding position zero-point-five klicks south of Hill 136." As she spoke, Weiss flicked her finger back and forth on the personal's papery expansion screen. Thousands of feet above them, a tiny drone hovered somewhere in the gusty emptiness of the open sky, rotors spinning silently. The craft was no bigger than a hummingbird, and it would be tilting and panning in concert with Weiss's finger moving on the screen.

"Eighty-two hours since touchdown. Situation is uneventful. Interlopers at Hill 136 are maintaining position zero-point-five klicks away in a hardened structure, position monitored by drone."

Weiss paused.

"Rations at 25%, equipage at 100% – fireteam status is hungry, but alert. Waiting on command touchdown for further instructions. Report time as zero-eight-zero-three. Nothing follows."

Weiss tugged on a corner of the expansion screen and it shrank, rasping itself back inside the personal's rubbery frame. Weiss's personal was the ruggedized military model handed out on their second day at Camp Albatross, while their civilian personals had been confiscated. The military's personals were not so different from the chunky, government-subsidized personal Eva had grown up with, but very unlike the slim, brushed-metal personals that her classmates had favored in school.

Weiss tucked her device into one of the many equipment pouches that rode on the skeletal frame of her battle jacket, and rolled over to face the sky. She tugged her rifle up to lay across her chest, and the weapon clanked against the green-painted steel of her battle jacket's chest piece.

"Did I say that right?"

Eva nodded.

"Very good. Very soldiery."

"How *sweet* of you," Weiss said, grinning. Eva's fireteam called her "Sweet," a shorthand for her surname, Sweetwater, and it had become an inside joke to exclaim, "How sweet of you!" whenever she did or said something even remotely kind. Eva made a show of rolling her eyes at Weiss, but privately, she felt warmed by the ease between them.

"My turn to keep tabs," Eva said.

She propped herself up on one elbow to rummage in her own battle jacket's chest pockets. The soft dirt of the trench wall yielded readily under her battle jacket's immense weight, and her steel-encased elbow sank several inches into the dirt. Trickles of cold pebbles and soil pattered through the battle jacket's struts and onto Eva's skin, a few bits catching fast in the crease of her elbow and the rolled-up sleeves of her uniform.

The battle jacket's armor covered the wearer's hand and fingers, but left the tips and fingernails exposed for fine motor tasks. She tugged her own militarized personal free and thumbed a few controls. An aerial view from the tiny drone's perspective appeared on the screen, showing meadows, rivers, and treetops like bushy green buttons on the landscape.

"How do you switch to thermal?"

"Double-tap on mode – a little box pops up and you can select it."

Another few taps from her thumb and the view shifted to dull grays and blacks with a tiny cluster of orange speckles. Eva tapped on the colorful dots and the view expanded, zooming in to show fiery, glowing human figures against a dark background, some sitting, some standing, some sleeping. They were enemy combatants, and a few held rifle-shaped blobs of dark color and looked outward from the group, or paced slowly along nearby hills. Several more gathered in a circle, orange and red limbs making eating motions.

"I count eight," Eva said.

"Yep."

"Did you see that they're eating?"

"Yep."

Eva's stomach grumbled as her fingernails found the edge of the pull tab for the personal's expansion screen. She tugged and it slid out, the display on the thin, crinkly sheet mirroring the image on the personal's smaller, glassy main display. She tapped and pinched a few times on the expanded screen, peering at the occasional speck of color.

"There's a deer or something near us," Eva said, eyeing a bright dot in a stand of small trees near to their trench, perhaps fifty yards away. "Oh, it's a wild pig."

Weiss tilted her head in thought. A soft gurgle emanated from her midsection.

"I'll shoot it, but I'm not touching it," she said airily. "Present me with carved hams after you deal with all the guts and such."

Eva chuckled.

"Speaking of ham," Weiss continued. "I think Sandy might be hiding some beans – the Cajun ones, with ham chunks."

She was eyeing Eva with playful nonchalance, but Eva had to suppress a small sigh before she responded. She and her fireteam had been holding position for nearly a week, with "holding position" being military parlance for sitting around, anxiously. After so much time spent holding position, Eva had heard enough bored jokes from her squadmates to last a lifetime, particularly when the jokes centered on Eva's love of the Cajun-style bean rations.

Nonetheless, she now understood that time went quicker talking with her fellow soldiers, about literally anything, than it went in silence. Time went quickest of all when she was talking to Weiss. In the shared misery of Camp Albatross, Weiss had shown herself to be witty, prickly, and frighteningly competent with a rifle. The stress of their training seemed to break over Weiss like waves on rock, leaving her unmarred. Occasionally, however, when it was just her and Eva, Weiss became secretly fragile in the way broken glass is fragile, glittering and jagged. She was Eva's favorite among her squadmates.

Weiss seemed to return the feeling, which still gave Eva a flicker of surprise. A teacher had once advised a young and tearful Eva that other children excluded her from their games because they found her "angry and quiet" – while true, this was not the entire story. In fact, the other kids had simply noticed the smell of a classmate who did not have running water in her house, and slotted Eva at the bottom of their tiny, childish caste system. From this, Eva learned early that feeling angry was much easier than feeling hurt.

At Camp Albatross, aggression was gleefully encouraged, particularly when paired with dispassion and a well-executed plan, and Eva was the most decorated recruit in her unit. She was closest with Weiss, but within the martial symbiosis of a soot group fireteam, she unexpectedly found herself with no shortage of good friends.

The feeling was unfamiliar and fantastic, so Eva shot her eyebrows dutifully skyward and leaned toward her friend, speaking in serious tones.

"You know how *I* feel about the Cajun beans."

"You and you alone." Weiss grinned.

"They wouldn't make them if nobody liked them!"

Weiss's gauntleted hand panned across the dirt of the trench wall until her fingertips found a small stone – she whipped it at Eva and it clinked off the armor plating of her battle jacket.

"If anyone still had some beans, it *would* be Sandy. Have you ever watched him savoring?"

Weiss sat up from where she lay against the trench's wall and struck a pose, closing her eyes in reverent bliss, bringing fingers to lips as though overcome by the decadence of some unseen flavor.

Eva giggled.

"So ... you think Sandy is pretty funny?"

"He's not, *not* funny," Weiss replied, giving her a very flat look.

Eva pursed her lips in feigned introspection.

"I think ... he also finds you not, *not* funny."

"I'm getting lost in the double negatives," Weiss replied. "But it sounds like you're saying he wants to rail me."

Eva shrugged cheerfully.

"Well, I'm not interested," Weiss said. "Not right now, anyway."

"Why not?"

"Have I told you about Lazlo and Caden?"

Eva shook her head.

"Well, I was dating Lazlo, who was thoughtful and very sexy. At the same time, I was cheating on him with Caden, who was *not* thoughtful but was *also* very sexy. Neither knew about the other. Okay so far?"

Eva nodded.

"Well, time passes and I start feeling worse and worse about it."

"As one does," Eva agreed, nodding affably, and Weiss laughed.

"Right, but I'm not feeling bad enough to *stop*, until one night I'm in bed with Caden, cheating on Lazlo, and suddenly I'm just not into it. At all."

Eva's eyebrows raised, and Weiss grinned.

"And it's not Caden – he's enthusiastic, doing everything the way I like, but this time ... I just feel nothing."

Weiss laid back against the dirt of the trench wall, folding her armor-gauntleted hands behind her helmet as she stared up at the sky.

"And he's *really* putting his back into it, to the point that it's getting awkward, and then ... I think about Lazlo. Because me and Lazlo used to be *great* in bed, but we weren't anymore, and that's probably what drove me to Caden in the first place. Even though he's worse than Lazlo in all kinds of ways."

Eva nodded.

"I think I was chasing that ... I don't know, sex spark? And then I start imagining that it's Lazlo, my actual boyfriend who I love, there in bed instead of Caden, the guy I'm cheating on him with. And then ..."

Weiss made an obscene gesture.

"... *voila*."

Eva buried her face in gauntleted hands, laughing. Weiss continued.

"So, I didn't enjoy sex with Lazlo *or* Caden, but I *did* enjoy sex with Caden as long as I *pretended* he was Lazlo. I decided that meant I wasn't mentally in the best place for a relationship, so I came clean and ended things with both of them. Which brings us to now, and Sandy, who I do find …"

"… not, *not* funny?" Eva supplied, and Weiss laughed.

"Exactly. Which is why I will *not* be doing anything with him. At least for now."

Sandy's voice crackled in Eva's ear.

"Outpost Bucket, send ack."

Weiss rocketed upright, her cheeks flushing.

"Ack, Outpost Piper. This is Sweet at Outpost Bucket," Eva responded, in a tone of excessive calm. Outpost Bucket was the fortified trench where she and Weiss were huddled, while Outpost Piper was a conference room inside a nearby abandoned office building, and currently represented their field headquarters.

"We need to regroup," Sandy continued. "Draw a cage around your interlopers and pull back to Outpost Piper. Canny?"

"Canny," Eva replied, tapping a few more times on the screen of her militarized personal, bringing the view back to the group of enemy combatants. She counted eight again, then used her finger to draw a boundary around the entire group. A green line followed her finger on the screen, enclosing the enemy troops in a clumsy lasso of color. The drone would already have alerted her if its reconnaissance algorithm decided that any of the figures were moving in ways that matched worrying patterns in its database, but now it would additionally alert her if any of the fiery figures crossed her traced boundary.

Weiss and Eva rose to a stooped stance that kept their helmets below the wall of the trench and disconnected their rifles from their chest pieces. Weighed down by dozens of equipment packs and several forms of direct and indirect weaponry, their hunched walk was nonetheless made effortless by the electroelastic muscles of the battle jackets that supported them from head to toe.

One of the trench's exits meandered away from the hill and into the edge of the town, eventually terminating as the low hill flattened onto an empty street lined with creaky buildings. They paused at the trench's exit, crouching together in the shelter of the low, receding dirt walls, and surveyed the quiet street for several moments. She would have liked to use another drone to check the surrounding streets for threats, but she and Weiss had only been issued one, and it was busy keeping an eye on the eight known threats half a klick away.

Instead, Weiss tapped the steel plating on Eva's armor and brought her rifle to her shoulder, resting the muzzle where it could fire on the empty street. Eva nodded, then hustled across the roadway in a running crouch. Her heart rate spiked as she left the trench's walls to cross the bare and cracked pavement, but the street offered no surprises or threats, and the only sound was the thuds of her sprinting feet.

She reached the nearest building, a brick structure three stories high and undifferentiable from the buildings that flanked it. It sat across the roadway from the exit to the trench, with an open doorway beckoning them into its dark interior. Eva sprinted to the edge of the doorframe, then paused and swept the muzzle of her rifle across the corners of the empty room. Finding no threats, she slipped inside and turned, raising her rifle to cover the street just as Weiss had done for her. She gestured and watched the empty roadway as Weiss sprinted across the street, and together they stacked up against a wall inside the doorframe.

The room was a lobby of sorts, a small space devoid of furniture and backed by doors to a stairwell and an elevator.

"Crumb for me, baby," Weiss said.

A moment passed, then Sandy's voice crackled from their helmet earpieces.

"Oh god, oh god, I'm gonna crumb."

Sandy had giggled for several hours after discovering that *"I'm gonna crumb"* could pass the profanity filters and be accepted as an official mission parameter. As a result, Fireteam Marko's mission plan stipulated that the phrase *"crumb for me, baby"* was code to indicate that friendlies were approaching an outpost, so the automated sentry turrets hidden at this building's access points needed to be shut down. *"Oh god, oh god, I'm gonna crumb"* was the rejoinder indicating that the turrets were safely deactivated, so she and Weiss could proceed.

Eva took one final look down the empty street, then followed Weiss through the door to the stairwell. Above them, a "glue gun" was fixed to the ceiling of the stairwell. Glue guns were automated sentry turrets about the size and shape of a pear, and contrary to their name, they did not shoot glue. Glue guns fired the same metallic slugs as Eva and Weiss's rifles, and got their name from a thick coat of gluey adhesive on one end that allowed them to be emplaced by simply hurling the device at a wall. The glue gun on the ceiling above Eva and Weiss had been mounted several days earlier by Sandy via that exact method.

On the second floor, they padded down a hallway that smelled dank with disuse, where one of the hallway doors was ajar to let another glue gun hidden inside strafe gunfire across any intruders. A few steps more and they found the conference room that served as Outpost Piper.

Outpost Piper was a large room but otherwise unimpressive – a pile of Fireteam Marko's meager supplies was stacked near one of the walls, and the space was brightly lit by large windows. Talk and Sandy looked up as Eva and Weiss entered, both sitting on the floor to keep themselves below the edge of the window frames. No one had been able to talk Sandy out of using a windowed room as a staging area, after the first few days spent staging out a humid interior office nearby.

"There's definitely someone out there – they're jamming us," Sandy said after nodding a greeting at them, his brow uncharacteristically furrowed. "Not all the time, just short bursts. Where's Uro?"

"We never saw her."

"Fuck."

Sandy and Talk both unclipped their rifles from their battle jackets.

"She said she was going to meet you at the trenches. Uro, send ack."

Eva's helmet earpiece was silent.

"Uro, mic check. We can't hear you. Send ack," Sandy said.

The silence in her earpiece seemed to become more pronounced. Several moments passed while Eva, Weiss, Sandy, and Talk all crouched in uncertain silence, hunkered below the windows of the conference room.

"Well, we need to see what's going on," Sandy said, and dug in an equipment pack on his hip.

He strode toward one of the conference room windows, pulling a small drone from his pack and unfolding its rotors and wings. He slid the window open and held the drone out above the empty street.

A gun drone, much larger than the tiny recon drone clutched in Sandy's fist, whirred lazily into view outside the window. Possibly attracted by the glinting of the glass as Sandy slid the window open, the gun drone was a tubular device slung under several rotors, like a stripped tree trunk carried by helicopters, all of it about the size of a dog. The gun drone studied Sandy, its sensors digesting data on his appearance, his equipment, and the entire context of the scene – all inputs to an onboard processor that churned constantly on grim calculations. The whole reckoning was solved in a few blips of electro-synaptic lightning, while Sandy's eyes were still wide with shock and he clutched his tiny, motionless recon drone in his outstretched fist.

The gun drone outside the window fired with a warbling shriek, sending a long burst of slugs into Sandy's chest. The window glass shattered under the assault and Sandy fell backward from the window, the armor of his chest piece splattered with vibrant blue.

Talk's hand was already at his belt. He drew a decoy flare and ignited it with a flick of his thumb, then whipped it out the window past the gun drone. The flare only fooled the drone for a moment, but it was enough time for Weiss to raise her rifle and fire. Eva realized her own rifle was already shouldered and squeezed the trigger. Their rifles issued the same chirruping scream as the gun drone's weapon and Eva felt the gun vibrate against her shoulder, a gentle susurration as it spit dozens of non-lethal training slugs per second, glazing the gun drone's hull with a slick coating of red dye. Defeated, the drone lowered obediently to the pavement outside.

Sandy was "dead" by the rules of the simulation and lay silently sprawled on the floor. The conference room of Outpost Piper was quiet in the aftermath of the gun drone's assault, and in the sudden silence, Eva's ears caught a faint whirring, like a desk fan in a distant room. She pulled her own flare from her belt just as a suicide drone fluttered into the room.

It was a pencil-sized device with tiny rotors, no larger or louder than a hummingbird — colloquially, the miniscule drones were called "flicks" and each had enough explosives to kill, or at least severely maim. Her flare sputtered to life, stinking smokily, and she flung it hard across the conference room. The flick darted to follow it, joined by two more of the devices that whizzed in from the hallway. Flicks were less intelligent than gun drones, having no data-hungry processors to suck in sensory data and decide between decoys and true threats, and all three of them piled onto the flare and detonated with cartoonish pops, spraying blue dye across the opposing wall of the conference room.

There would be a second, much larger group of flicks only a few seconds away — they were released as a swarm that divided up to check all rooms and floors simultaneously. The bulk of that swarm would now be zipping eagerly toward the sound of their exploded compatriots.

"Turn on the glue guns!" Eva shouted, and as she did, she realized that re-activating the little pear-shaped sentry turrets would likely not be enough to keep her fireteam from "dying."

They had yet to see a human attacker, but the timing and sequence of the drone assault had been exacting. Her fireteam's glue guns were an effective countermeasure to flicks, and would have gunned down the little suicide drones as they entered the building. Therefore, the attacking swarm of flicks had been released within the short window of opportunity when Weiss and Eva entered the building, and requested that the glue guns be deactivated.

Their attackers had silently eliminated Uro, purposefully allowed Eva and Weiss to enter the building unharmed, and then come close to wiping their entire fireteam using nothing more than careful timing and a handful of flicks. The gun drone outside the window had also been well-timed – if Sandy had not surprised it by opening the window, it would have opened fire right as the flicks first found them, splitting her fireteam's attention and most likely assuring their defeat.

Eva pulled another decoy flare and held it nervously. They had survived the first drone assault, but Fireteam Marko had still lost two of its five members without even seeing an enemy in-person.

Talk had already retrieved his personal to re-activate the glue guns as Weiss pulled a fresh glue gun from her own pack, ripped the paper off its adhesive bottom, and hurled it out the open door to the conference room.

Weiss's glue gun stuck to the wall outside and immediately began swatting down a swarm of flicks that had appeared in the hallway outside, firing its tiny gun barrel with a pitchy screech. Eva heard the drones' rotors clack and skitter to a halt on the floor outside, nearly a dozen of them piling up dead outside the doorway to their conference room. A single drone penetrated the glue gun's hail of slugs, whizzing inside the conference room to detonate on top of Weiss in a spray of blue dye before Eva had the chance to thumb the igniter on her flare. Weiss's battle jacket deactivated and she crumpled to the floor, "dead."

Moments later, the glue gun in the hallway stopped firing, and in the quiet that followed Eva no longer heard the telltale whirring of drone rotors. Their as-yet-unseen attackers had now killed three out of five members of Fireteam Marko, but for the moment at least, they seemed to be out of drones.

She and Talk locked eyes.

"I think this is going pretty well," she said.

The corpses of Weiss and Sandy snickered, and Talk grinned.

"They've got to be out of drones now, but they're watching the windows. Probably the hallway, too. Should we barricade the door?" he asked.

"They'll just put grenades through the window," she said. "No reason for them to risk a push, they know where we are and they can see our exits."

Motty often told them, "If the enemy has an edge, dull it." This enemy appeared to have many advantages, but their knowledge of Eva and Talk's location was one that could be removed – they needed to move.

Their glue gun, however, was complicating things. It would protect them if more drones arrived, but as long as they kept it online it was also trapping her and Talk. Like the flicks, it was a small, simple device and could not interpret friend from foe, so it would fire on them the moment they left the conference room.

"Follow me."

Eva stood and sprinted toward the end of the conference room, away from the hallway door. She lowered her shoulder and smashed through the interior wall, letting the armor plating and electroelastic muscles of the battle jacket carry her well into the adjoining room in a shower of dusty fiberboard scraps and puffs of pink, cottony insulation. The adjoining room was a small kitchenette with a sink and moldering cabinets, but Eva barely noticed as she carried her momentum into a powerful sprint.

She dropped her shoulder again and crashed her armored body through the kitchenette's far wall, demolished the smooth white fiberboard as she burst into a third room – a small office. She was paralleling the hallway, and crossed the room with three long strides before slamming her shoulder through the opposite wall once again, emerging into yet another decrepit office space in a final spray of architectural debris.

She shook her head to clear the trickles of chalky dust from her helmet and surveyed the final room – it was a window office at the end of the hall, just as she had hoped. Talk arrived behind her, accompanied by a crunching, trickling noise as bits of ravaged wall panel fell away around the ragged hole made by their passage.

Eva paused only for a moment to survey the street for threats, then dove out the window.

Her stomach looped and whirled as she plummeted from the second story and hit the ground with an enormous thud, her battle jacket's leg struts absorbing the immense impact but still cracking the sidewalk beneath her. She heard Talk land behind her and together they sprinted across the street away from Outpost Piper. She waited for the screech of enemy rifles to sing out as they moved across the bare pavement, but it didn't come, and she and Talk barreled into the building across the street, still sprinting.

36 days before

———•———

"**WE CAN'T** take Hill 136 with two of us any better than we could with all five of us," Eva said. "So, the mission is the same – we need to wait for reinforcements and instructions."

"How do we know they won't find us again? They found us last time."

"That's because Sandy put us next to a window," Eva replied. "I think if they knew where we were, they'd have finished us off by now."

They were crouched together in an office tucked at the corner of an empty warehouse, five blocks from the office building that once housed Outpost Piper. It was a clean but small room, with a long, low window ideal for surveying the warehouse floor, and absolutely no exterior windows.

Talk knelt at the edge of the windowsill.

"I'll take first watch," he said.

Eva smiled thanks and sat against the wall of the office, moving slowly to keep her battle jacket's armor plating from clanking against the office's thin metal wall. She was sitting for almost a minute before she realized her hands were shaking. She swallowed hard and wished for water.

"You feeling wobbly, too?" Talk asked, quietly.

She looked at him in surprise. He looked poised as he knelt at the window, statuesque inside his battle jacket's bulky frame.

"My knees won't stop shaking inside the armor," he said helpfully, and Eva sighed with relief.

"I thought it was just me. I know it's just a simulation, but ... they *died*. It was so fast, we never even *saw* the enemy, just their drones. Is that how it will be?"

"I think it might be," he said, sounding troubled. "Not very heroic, for them or us."

"Think Weiss and Sandy and Uro are still laying there?" she asked.

"For two hours. That's how long Chief Marko said the armor locks up for. They'll still be eating a hot meal before we will, though."

As they talked, Eva noticed that her hands were still shaking, but less with each passing minute.

"Change shifts every hour?" she asked.

Talk nodded, then abruptly began digging in his hip pack. A moment later he tossed something to her, and she gasped as she caught it. It was a can of beans with a black label – Cajun-style. Eva loved each of the four flavors of beans common in Rugeran meal kits, but Cajun was the most precious.

"I set this can aside before we realized our food would run out," Talk said. "But then it didn't feel right to eat it by myself, after everyone else was going hungry. Now that it's just two of us, though, might as well not be scared *and* hungry."

"Why didn't you eat it before? Too spicy?"

"No, I love it. The Cajun-style are the best beans."

Eva's eyes shone with emotion.

"So, why not eat them?"

"I guess I thought we all could share them, like a party. Cajun is most people's favorite flavor, so everyone eats it right away, but if I saved some, and we all had a bite or two together ... I don't know. *Party* is the wrong word."

Talk spoke without looking at her, still keeping watch on the empty warehouse floor.

"A *gathering*, maybe? But that sounds like we're witches. It's just ... we've been out here so long, but I actually like it, these extended exercises where it's just our fireteam by ourselves, solving problems and watching each other's back."

Talk shrugged, and the huge, armored shoulders of his battle jacket shrugged with him.

"We're all bored out here, so I just thought if I saved a can in the special flavor everyone likes, we could share it one night."

Eva set the can of beans down next to her.

"That's a nice thought, Talk. But you're making me feel bad, because I ate my Cajun beans the first time we stopped to eat."

Talk gave a muffled laugh, and the empty warehouse swallowed the sound.

"And you're right – it is nice, being out here," she continued. "Also, this may be the most I've ever heard you say at once."

He nodded affably.

"I like everyone in our fireteam, but I've never been big on talking in groups. Are you?"

"Do I seem like I am?"

Talk gave her a sidelong glance.

"Hard to say. You can be pretty bubbly," he said, smiling. "But not all the time. Sometimes I think you're a little like me – more comfortable being alone."

A pleasant prickling radiated under her skin. She had been watching Talk, but had not known that he was watching her, in return.

She grinned at him. "Say more things that you think about me."

"Hmmm." Talk was quiet for several moments. "I think of you like … a beach ball. I don't know how else to say it – like someone was holding a beach ball underwater, and finally let go, and now you're bursting out of the water. Into the sun."

Eva was quiet for several long moments, and Talk looked at her uneasily.

"I'm sorry. This is why I don't talk a lot, I always—"

"—you're okay," she said, smiling slowly. "That was just … I didn't know I was so transparent."

"You're not!" Talk continued to look worried. "I don't think anyone else … noticed. Not that I'm even right about anything – it was just a silly thought I had."

"It's not that silly," she said, after studying him in the quiet of the empty warehouse for several moments. "School wasn't much fun for me, so I kept to myself a lot. But then I got here, and all this …" Eva gestured to the rifle across her chest, and the armor they both wore. "… feels so easy, by comparison. And everyone on our team is so nice."

She paused, swallowing.

"You're right, I'm most comfortable when I'm alone. But maybe before I came here, alone time wasn't really a choice, it was just something that happened. Now, I can choose between being alone, or not. And I guess I really like that."

It was Talk's turn to be quiet for several moments before he spoke.

"I know exactly what you mean," he said at last.

An oddly comfortable silence stretched between them. Eva let it linger in space as she relaxed into her seat against the wall, and Talk continued to keep watch at the window.

* * * * * * * * * *

Minutes passed, turning into hours. They swapped places at the office's low window every so often, and the day drew towards afternoon.

"Bean time?" she asked, and he grinned.

"I did mean to share with the whole group, but if I can only share it with one other person, it should be you. You *really* like the Cajun-style, right?"

Eva felt a blush rise in her cheeks and nodded. She popped the lid of the can and dropped a heat pea inside – a small, taut ball of white fabric no larger than its namesake. A minute or so later, steam began to rise from the mixture of sauce and beans.

She and Talk passed the warm can back and forth, tipping it up and letting the beans run into their mouths in small gulps that spilled hot, sticky sauce on their lips.

Outside, the afternoon sun decayed to a cool, dark night that filled the echoing confines of the old warehouse. They had no more drones to scout the area, and the night seemed oddly heavy, less a fading of the light than an inrush of dismal, tangible dark.

More hours passed, and Eva now knelt at the windowsill as Talk dozed, gazing out across a warehouse interior gone completely black. Even in the dark, she could keep watch on the bare floor and distant doorways through goggles that slid down from her helmet's brow. The warehouse was displayed in crisp detail inside the goggles, illuminated with a gray, powdery light by the helmet's night vision amplifier.

Talk's chest rose and fell as he breathed, deep and slow respirations that Eva did her best to match whenever a distant clanging from a rusty road sign or wailing from the windy street sent her nerves skittering.

Abruptly, a voice crackled over her helmet's earpiece.

"Message to Fireteam Marko. Abort mission and return to base. The hostiles at Hill 136 have been neutralized by other means."

The message repeated itself three times as Eva knelt, stunned, at the windowsill. Talk, no longer asleep, began to laugh.

When they returned to Camp Albatross, Drill Instructor Motty explained that they had completed Low Intensity Sustained Tactical Readiness (LISTR) training, and since at least 40% of their fireteam's strength remained following the ambush, they had passed. Both the week spent holding position and the subsequent ambush were intended to test them against a soldier's most persistent foe – boredom. Motty screamed criticisms of their performance at them individually, of course, before grudgingly acknowledging that Talk and Eva's successful evasion of the ambush team had been instrumental in obtaining a passing grade.

Motty then admitted that LISTR was the final exercise necessary before graduation – Fireteam Marko had completed basic training. They would be rewarded with several days of personal leave, then join Chief Marko as full-fledged soldiers.

33 days before

EVEN BURIED in the damp warmth of a crowded dance floor, Uro and her wife, Rochelle, drew onlookers from every floor of the club. Uro was short, and two months of daily exercise at Camp Albatross had wrapped her in ropy muscle, while Rochelle was contrastingly tall with a face that could be readily described as angelic. Her mismatch to Uro was almost as eye-catching as the gleeful elasticity of their twirls and jolts on the floor. They looked like two souls resonating as one, giving off a contented glow as they did.

"Rochelle is stupidly pretty," Eva said, talking loud over the throbbing music.

Weiss blew out a sigh and nodded in agreement. They leaned against a railing of boxy steel and dark wood on the second floor, overlooking the dance floor. Their elbows were touching, and the porous, grainy timber of the railing was warm under their elbows from the breathy air inside the club.

"I kind of knew she'd be hot," Weiss said. "Maybe I didn't expect she'd be *that* pretty, but something about Uro, you know? Like, I'm not that surprised. You can just *look* at Uro and know she must fuck like a stick of dynamite."

Eva guffawed, the noise loud even over the club's music, and a nearby boy wearing only skin-tight capri pants gave her a strange look. Eva took a bracing drink from her cup – the liquor was dry and sweet.

"Maybe they're just in love, and who's pretty or good in bed doesn't matter so much," she replied.

"They met when they were little," Talk interjected, leaning against the railing nearby. "They got separated for a few years, then found each other again. I don't know where or when they got married, but they had to go overspace to do it. She said they're going back to wherever it was, maybe even emigrating formally, once her duty tour is over."

"Just love can't maintain a couple who looks that different." Weiss managed to sound airy even though she was almost shouting to be heard over the music. "If Uro's not great in bed, maybe Rochelle needs citizenship, or something like that. There's a thing going on there, I know it. It can't be just love."

"That's a depressing take," Talk replied, his tone noncommittal. "And besides, I think they *both* look great."

The three of them watched Uro and Rochelle twirl on the dance floor below. It was several seconds before Weiss spoke again.

"Okay, it's not *just* because Rochelle is so pretty, she could be ugly as long as she had money or something. People who are rich, or who look like *that*—"

She pointed her finger at Rochelle, still dancing giddily with Uro a floor below them.

"—can't trust that they're genuinely loved, unless the other person is also beautiful, or rich, or both. Love doesn't conquer a fundamental power imbalance."

There was a pause then where the music throbbed and Weiss took a small, angry sip from a bottle of clear liquor with elegant black script on the label. Eva exchanged a bemused look with Talk, then leaned toward him, confident the blaring music around them would mask her words from Weiss.

"I think she's just grumpy because of *that*."

She and Talk followed Weiss's gaze down to another part of the dance floor, where Sandy danced with a girl in a clinging, backless dress. Sandy's shirt was open down to his stomach in the current style, and the girl's back was pressed against his chest, skin to skin, with her skirt rucked up around her thighs so they could move in sync to impulsive music.

Talk opened his mouth to reply but was interrupted when a smiling girl appeared next to him. Her blouse was thin, and her skirt was short. Talk smiled back, and the girl leaned in close. Eva realized she was craning her neck to catch their conversation over the thumps of music and burbles of the crowd, and made herself stop. A moment later, the thin-bloused girl laughed, high and enthusiastic, and Eva's eyes narrowed.

A boy in a tight-fitting shirt appeared next to her and Weiss, cutting the two of them off from Talk and the laughing girl. The boy's smile was white and the stubble that crawled over his jaw was trimmed in laser-straight lines.

"You ladies thirsty?" The question was directed at neither of them in particular.

Eva raised her half-full cup, warding him off. Weiss watched Sandy for a few moments more, her elbows still on the railing, before turning her slim neck to regard the boy over one shoulder left bare by her dress. Their eyes locked, and the grinning boy stepped closer to her.

"What you got in the bottle? Need another?"

"It's water," Weiss said, her tone dull.

"Let me buy you something yummy."

Eva suppressed a small shudder and Weiss studied the boy wordlessly. The moment stretched, the silence becoming uneasy as Eva and the boy in the tight shirt both realized that although Weiss's mind was churning, it did not churn for him.

"I don't drink," she said at last and turned back to the dance floor. She took another sip from the bottle, and the boy left.

Talk stood alone once again – the laughing girl had been only the most recent of a line of glittering club-goers to excitedly swirl around him, before he gently dismissed them to continue chatting with her and Weiss.

"Is that really just water? You don't like alcohol?"

Eva spoke after realizing she had been staring at Talk for a half-breath too long, and turned her eyes back to the flailing, eclectically-lit circus of the dance floor.

"I didn't say I don't *like* it. I just don't *drink* it."

Weiss's tone was bland and aloof, and the skin around Eva's eyes tightened as a burst of hot impatience oozed under her skin. She was no stranger to Weiss's moodiness – she normally adored the quicksilver intensity of her friend's energy, cycling from petty to devoted to anxious and back, sometimes in a matter of minutes – but tonight the liquor in Eva's stomach was sapping her patience. She considered several needling retorts regarding Sandy's appalling failure to drag himself around in Weiss's footsteps, licking the ground she walked on, and took another pull from her cup to buy herself time to choose.

As she brought the cup back down, she felt a sway in her head as the liquor jostled her vision, and before she could speak Talk stepped closer to her.

"Want to go dance with me?"

One hand was outstretched to her, while the other held his own cup. His shirt was open to the stomach, like Sandy's, and months of daily exercise showed in the lines of his bare chest and stomach, lit by a gleam of sweat. He had drunk enough that his eyes were bright and his smile a bit lopsided, which struck Eva as shatteringly steamy.

His hand was warm as it closed around hers, and she realized belatedly that she had already held it out to him. They took several strides toward the stairs to the dance floor before Eva paused, and Talk stopped alongside at the tug of her hand.

Weiss was alone against the railing, in a thin dress with clinging tights the same color and shine as fresh snow. It made Eva furious to see her friend by herself, refusing to look at them, shoulders set meekly above legs as long and bright as fangs. They were soot group: the smartest, fastest, and most vicious of all Ruger's military, and they had seventy-two hours of leave.

"WEISS!" Eva shrieked the name, slopping some of her drink out of its cup and onto the club's floor.

"You are *so pretty*! You are tall and strong, like bamboo!" The alcohol was garbling her speech and the last word sounded a bit like "blam-bloo" but Weiss's face still warmed into a smile. Next to Eva, Talk giggled.

Eva tipped her cup upward, downing the rest of her drink. Gulped in such quantity, the sweetness was overwhelmed by the stinging burn of alcohol in her nose.

"Let's go dance!" Eva shouted, and Weiss capped her water bottle and bounded to meet them, legs flashing under the dim gleam of the club's lights.

33 days before

―――――――――◆●―――――――――

SANDY WALKED with the taut but wobbly confidence of a young person with alcohol in their belly and a crotch that had been briefly and consensually rubbed by a stranger. He tapped at his personal – Chief Marko had returned the devices to them for the space of their short leave.

"What's the app called?" Uro asked.

"*The bone life*," Sandy snickered unaffectedly. "She said it's because everyone uses it to bone."

Uro leaned to look at the screen of Sandy's personal as they walked.

"I think it's pronounced *bonne*, Sandy. It's French for 'good.' Like, *the good life*."

Sandy was too immersed in the app to hear.

"What? Create a profile? Why? Just let me in," Sandy's fingernail clicked on the screen as he stabbed it in annoyance. "Skip. Skip. Skip. Set my background color? Fine, blue. Great job? I don't need this praise."

"Don't those apps just match you with random people? How will you find her?"

Rochelle, Uro's wife, looked on with interest over Uro's shoulder, their hands intertwined as they kept pace with Sandy.

"Not random. Don't need to match," Sandy shook his head vehemently. "Don't need to. I got it all set up. She gave me her profile, so I just find her and ..."

One more tap of his finger, this one particularly resounding.

"... *bonne*."

Eva watched jealousy flash across Weiss's face, masked almost instantly by dull irritation. She and Eva walked a few feet behind, hands clutched to their elbows, shoulders tilted toward one another so that the skin of their upper arms could rub together, sharing warmth. Glittery flaps of their dresses fluttered as a chilled, oily wind sloughed down the city street, and Eva wished she had thought to print a cardigan. She and Weiss had printed their outfits only hours before, using their hotel's public printer and outfit templates that they each kept saved on their personals.

A steady stream of cars burbled by, quietly methodical, as shouting masses of young partyers crowded the sidewalk. Eva's shoes sent a fresh spike of pain up her leg as someone bumped her and sent her stumbling. Weiss's arm snaked out to steady her, but as Eva looked up to thank her, she saw a faint sneer in her friend's eyes.

Eva's own eyes narrowed and she pushed Weiss into a passing alley, a dim space bare of bystanders. She marched them a dozen steps into the dimness, abruptly unwilling to tolerate the noise of the late-night street crowd, until she and Weiss were alone.

"Will you cut it out tonight?"

Weiss cocked her head as she regarded Eva.

"Cut what out?" Her tone was placid and bored.

"Oh, fuck off, Weiss." Eva paused and burped quietly. The air in her throat tasted like potato wine, and she gave her friend a small, fussy shove.

"I'm trying here, and I want you to try, too! We've only got a few nights to have fun!"

Weiss rolled her eyes.

"Worry about yourself."

"No, Weiss. I will worry about *you*, because you're being cranky and I am trying to understand where my friend has gone, and why *this* asshole is standing here instead."

Eva gestured snappily, and the jerky movement exposed the sweat in her armpits to the chilled night air. Weiss seemed to soften at the performance, but still said nothing.

"Just tell him," Eva said at last, her voice low, not far above a whisper. "He worships you."

Weiss shook her head.

"If you made a pass, Sandy'd throw that girl from the club into traffic to get to you."

Weiss laughed, but eyed Eva skeptically.

"Really?"

"Definitely."

Weiss rolled her shoulders and leaned against the alley wall, the gossamer material of her dress catching against the cold, craggy bricks.

"It's just not the right time," she said at last. "Not only for me. For him, either."

Eva squinted her eyes, wordlessly prompting.

"I know he's great. Underneath all the peacocking, I *like* Sandy, I really do."

Weiss's eyes were black and featureless in the dimness of the alley.

"But boys are kind of like fruit – they have to ripen. Bite into them too early, and they can be nasty. Or bland. Or both. And once you bite, it's over. Can't put bitten fruit back."

Eva paused, taking longer to absorb her friend's metaphor than she would have two drinks ago.

"So, how long?" she asked at last.

Weiss shook her head sagely.

"I don't know. It's not an age thing. I've known a lot of guys, even older guys, even *much* older guys, who were still ... unripe. And I'm still working through my own stuff, after Lazlo and Caden, so I'll just wait."

Eva nodded vaguely, unconvinced but suddenly too tired to be anything but agreeable. She puffed out a sigh and leaned one shoulder against the wall next to Weiss. The cold of the bricks sliced through her dress at once, and she wondered how Weiss didn't shiver.

"It must suck to watch him with other girls, in the meantime," she said slowly. "But will you please stop being mean to *me* about it?"

Weiss saddened.

"I'm sorry. I'll be better, I promise," she paused and looked even sadder. "But ... do you think he's going to fuck that girl? From the club?"

Eva hugged her friend, their skin pressing together warmly under the wind that sluiced down the alley.

"Of course not," she said. "And you're prettier than her, anyway."

Weiss giggled with pleasure and Eva moved away from the wall, tugging her back toward the crowded street.

"Come on, we'll trash his personal so he can't talk to anyone but us. Problem solved, for tonight at least."

"Is that too mean?" Weiss asked.

"He'll just get another tomorrow. They're cheap around here."

"Wait."

Weiss's hands resisted Eva's pull, bringing them face-to-face in the dim alleyway.

"My turn for advice," she said, her eyes once again bright but colorless in the shades of night around them.

"I don't think you should go for it, with Talk."

Eva's face collapsed with abrupt, all-consuming despair.

"Why-yyyyyyyyy?" she drew the sound out whinily.

Weiss paused and opened her mouth long before she spoke, as though gathering her words with care.

"So, he's extremely cute."

Eva nodded so hard that her vision shook.

"And I think he likes you," Weiss continued.

Eva squealed and squished her hands into balls, burrowing into herself happily. Weiss laughed and put her hands on Eva's shoulders.

"But look, he's just trouble, okay? I mean, he's a good guy, right down to his bones. That's the problem, though, he's *too* nice. You'll be asking him whether to vacation at the beach or in the mountains, and he's going to put his hand on your arm and say …"

Weiss deepened her voice and spoke somberly.

"… Eva, light of my life, moon of my stars, I want us to live in a grass hut in Ufpolan, to save some species of weird bird. It's just for three years. Why are you crying? And you'll shut it down, obviously, but it'll take forever and he'll be so sad about it, and then the birds will actually die, and it'll be on the news, and then he'll see it and—"

"—Miss?"

The voice was whispery, ragged, and disturbingly close – it seemed to emanate from a low pile of garbage nearby in the alley. Weiss and Eva started as the mound of dark refuse shifted, then rose to its feet, becoming a huge man in ratty clothing that towered over them in the night.

"Miss, can I ask you a question?"

His faint scrape of a voice was mismatched to the gargantuan size of him, which was now blocking them off from the lively street beyond the alley. With a scuff of a shoe against pavement in the cool night, a woman appeared behind Eva and Weiss in the same instant. Her face was spectrally thin and she dressed the same as the man – worn and mismatched, but layered, as if they planned to spend too much time outside. Together they were quiet as mice, but untimid.

"We don't have any cash," Eva said. The streets around the club were littered with beggars – they had been stopped a dozen times that day.

"He didn't ask you for money," the woman said, her voice even more ghostly than the man's.

"Yeah, I didn't ask," he echoed.

Eva, having spoken last, became their focus.

"I just want to ask you a question," the man repeated, and shuffled a step toward her. He stood a full head above her, so Eva had to crane her neck to look into the dark hood around his face.

"We're going back to our friends," Weiss said, and began walking briskly toward the edge of the alley to get around the man.

As she did, she caught Eva's stare and her eyes were wide. Eva had seen Weiss while sleeping, while vomiting, while laughing, and while firing a rifle. She had seen her in moods ranging from elated to vengeful to disinterested. This was the first time she had seen Weiss afraid.

"No!"

The thin woman's voice was high and anxious, and she looked from them to the man and back as though she expected some action from him. When he only stood inert, she darted forward, putting herself next to him and between Eva, Weiss, and the crowded street.

A small silver knife appeared in her hand, and Eva felt her stomach get very cold. Another knife came out of the man's pocket – the blade seemed laughably small in his huge fist. He held it tightly but still did not move, and in the damp light of the alleyway, a glittering from the blade telegraphed that his huge hands were trembling.

The sight of the knives sent Camp Albatross surging through Eva, smashing aside the liquor in her blood and replacing it with cold readiness that tensed her muscles and adjusted her stance. Her mouth was dry and her skin was chilled by the cool night wind, but she did not shake, only tightened her hands into fists.

"Give us your personals, and your purses," the woman said in her faint, scratchy voice, and gestured with her knife at the clutches Eva and Weiss each held. Eva saw Weiss's mouth flatten into a line and her friend stepped in front her, placing herself between Eva and their two attackers.

"Okay," Weiss said the word in a soothing monotone, then thrust her hand backward toward Eva, gesturing for her clutch.

They could scream for help, of course, but Eva knew they were in no real danger, not with the passersby on the street so close. There might be blood, there might be stitches, but Eva had endured those many times at Camp Albatross. She and Weiss knew how to control an opponent's knife and keep the blade away from their own flesh. They knew that if they had to take a cut, to take it on their chest, where ribs and collarbone would armor their bodies and produce a slash wound that bled but did not kill.

Eva heard Weiss's breath quicken in front of her, and from somewhere vicious inside her, a thought oozed darkly into being – she and Weiss did not have to surrender anything to these robbers, because she and Weiss could kill them, instead.

They might be bleeding at the end of it, but there was no doubt in Eva's mind that she and Weiss would be the victors. Two on two, and the woman looked reedy and weak under her thick clothes while the man's will was clearly not behind his knife. She and Weiss would go for the eyes – the man might be twice their size and armed, but no one does anything but shield themselves once a fingernail pushes past the skin of their eyelid. The hand-to-hand dummies at Camp Albatross had spaces inside the head where oranges could be stuffed behind the dummy's eye sockets. An orange, Motty said, was an excellent mimic of a human eyelid and eyeball, and their fast, gouging thumbs had produced sprays of citrus as they practiced.

A dark, hot puddle of rage began to pool inside Eva as she stared at the huge man and the rail-thin woman, still brandishing their knives. They had waited in this alley, armed and eager, hoping to see fear bloom in her face. They wanted to take what was not theirs. They wanted to make her feel helpless. They wanted to leave her in tears.

The rage inside her began to boil, flushing her face hot, burning away the chill of the cool air inside the dark alleyway. She and Weiss could surrender their clutches. She and Weiss could scream for help. Or, she and Weiss could kill them. The man and the woman had knives, but thanks to Camp Albatross, Eva and Weiss were the ones in control.

She, Eva, was in control.

It felt fantastic.

The heat inside her cooled to readiness, smooth and sharp, but a footstep splashed in a gritty puddle before she could move – it was all the warning anyone had before Sandy tackled the thin woman from behind. He let out a victorious grunt, sending both of them tumbling in front of the massive man, who still held his knife outstretched.

Weiss screeched and dove after him, and Eva's heart sank – on the ground and distracted, Weiss and Sandy were now in real danger. She kept her eyes locked to the dark hood of the man, willing him not to move, not to plunge the gleaming knife into her friends' exposed backs and drag the blade back out again, rising and falling, red and wet.

"It's three on two now, and you're holding that knife incorrectly," she spoke clearly and firmly, fighting the urge to babble. She kept her face serene and her gaze fixed on the massive, hooded man.

He stayed motionless for several moments, watching silently from inside his hood, still holding the knife in his outstretched hand. Without a word, he began to advance toward the tumult of wrestling limbs that was Sandy, Weiss, and the woman dressed in rags.

Eva did not remember moving, but she must have. She did not remember reaching for his knife, but she must have. Her rage had crystallized into something black and gleaming, carved to same size and shape as her need to keep Weiss and Sandy safe.

It put strength behind her hands, and strategy behind her attack. A pincer grip on the huge man's wrist, her fingers like steel bands, twisting. Capturing the skin-warmed handle of his knife in her own palm. Stripping it away from him as he grunted in surprise.

The thrust was almost unintentional. Like dotting the period at the end of a sentence, it had already happened before she thought to do it. Natural. Necessary. The knifepoint parted the fabric of the huge man's shirt, and Eva imagined popping sounds, as if she could hear each thread of fabric yielding under pressure and steel until the blade found warm flesh beneath, and then, kept going.

The huge man stopped all at once, as though frozen in time. He made a strange, soft sound – a sort of whispering exhale – as she pulled the knife from his stomach.

The second thrust was a surprise even to Eva. Two inches down and one inch to the left. The knife went inside the man a second time, and again he blew out that odd, desperate breath.

The third thrust was clean, almost clinical. People who cared for her were in danger, and this is how she would make them safe. Sandy and Weiss would do the same for her – she was certain of it. That certainty had become the answer to a question Eva realized she had been asking the world since she was a child.

The question had no words, just shape and gravity – a heavy ache at the center of her – but tonight she finally had an answer.

She was not alone.

She was not ignored.

She could be loved.

And when necessary, she could be feared.

Eva blinked, and her moment of reverie snapped into clarity.

Something was wrong – the huge man was frozen in place but still standing, silent and clearly not at a level of distress commensurate with three stab wounds. She skipped backward, light on the balls of her feet, putting distance between her and the grasp of those massive fingers. Knife at the ready.

Behind her, Sandy was hanging on to the ragged woman's wrist to keep her knife's blade controlled, while Weiss kicked her over and over in the ribs. At last, the woman dropped her knife and crawled away to sit by the huge man's tree-like leg. He watched the three of them from inside his hood, wavering slightly on his feet but otherwise showing no signs of wear.

Sandy was panting on the ground with Weiss standing over him, brandishing the woman's dropped knife, when the huge man bent and dragged his partner to her feet. Both limping slightly, they sidled around Eva and her friends to retreat into the dim alley, disappearing as quietly as they had arrived.

Eva breathed out slowly, through her nose.

Weiss and Sandy were sitting together in the gritty wet of the alley floor as Weiss poked and fussed at him, her fingers prodding for blood or wounds. Sandy was quiet throughout the examination, his smile broad and lopsided from alcohol, enjoying her attention immensely.

"You good, Sweet?" Weiss paused to eye Eva with concern.

Eva nodded, and Weiss turned back to Sandy with her eyebrows tight in annoyance.

"You shouldn't have let yourself get so close to her," she growled at him.

"I liked the part where you were worried about me."

"Yes." Weiss's tone was imperious. "You did a very stupid thing, and it worried me. Gleamers are the worst kind of addict – they don't feel pain and they would have gutted you neck to nuts for pocket change."

A black streak of worry lanced through Eva. If he did not feel pain, would the huge man even realize he needed a doctor? Or would he simply keep walking – bleeding, and bleeding, and bleeding – until there was no blood left to lose? She had only meant to protect Weiss and Sandy. But now, somewhere in the murky sprawl of the city, would that man die because of her?

"I saved you!" Sandy said it with conviction.

"We were fine," Weiss replied. "Sweet didn't even need help with the big guy. *You* needing saving, because you're drunk and fought stupid."

Sandy pondered this for several moments.

"I saw a knife. I really didn't want them to hurt you," he said, with the frankness of heavy inebriation. "So, I *tackled* her."

He grinned broadly.

Weiss was silent but put her hands out to help him stand. Sandy grabbed her eagerly, but only held on, making no move to lift himself. They froze for just a moment, eyes locked to each other with their fingers interlaced.

"I'm in love with you, Weiss."

She rolled her eyes.

"You're drunk, Sandy."

"I'm both!" He was indignant.

Weiss ignored Sandy's outburst and cast another look at Eva.

"You're *sure* you're good, Sweet? That guy was huge."

"I'm fine. Once I took his knife, he got scared and backed off right away."

The lie had left her mouth, smooth and certain, before she even recognized the words as false.

"No big deal," she finished weakly, then smiled at her friend as she tucked the knife against her side, where the dark of the alley would hide the blood.

Weiss left Sandy's side in an instant, appearing in front of Eva and sending a strange, sudden terror flooding through her. In the midst of Eva's struggle with the huge man, she had felt a burst of rich certainty that her fireteam would do anything to protect her, just as she would for them.

Now, in the odd calm of the aftermath, that certainty curdled and she pressed the bloody knife deeper into the cloth of her dress, willing Weiss not to notice it. She had stabbed a man three times – a man she had never met, never hated, never wished dead – and each thrust had been more forceful than the last. It was not normal. It was not likable. It was jagged and secret and wrong.

She was a freak.

And everyone was about to see it.

Weiss grabbed Eva's chin, fingers clamping her cheek. Eva could not see her expression in the dimness, until a stray moonbeam shone on Weiss's teeth. Her friend was grinning at her, bright and fierce, and just like that Eva's world stopped unraveling.

Weiss spoke in a whisper.

"If you're telling me that guy ran off, no muss no fuss, then that's what happened. I'll swear to anyone, understand?"

Weiss jostled Eva's head gently, fingers still biting into her chin, locking their faces close together.

"When I saw those knives, all I could think was how fucking happy I was that it was you, out of everyone else, here to back me up."

Eva blinked hard and nodded, willing her expression to stay even. Inside, a wave of relief was stealing the air from her lungs, making her want to gasp, to cry, to collapse into a puddle and have her friend hold her.

Weiss knew. She knew what Eva had done to protect her and Sandy, or at least, she suspected. Yet, she was not horrified, not even curious.

She was grateful.

Weiss kissed Eva's forehead, her lips hard and wet, then released her grip on Eva's chin. Eva took a deep, steady breath, and Weiss flashed her one more smile, then bounded back to Sandy.

"And if you're so *in love* with me, why were you loudly trying to fuck that girl from the club?" she snapped at him, all friendliness leaving her tone at once.

"To make you jealous," Sandy replied, squinting at her and speaking in a tone of earnest confusion, prompting Eva to wonder if the liquor in his brain had informed him that such a strategy would be both obvious and compelling.

Weiss's face did something strange, and Eva wondered if the same thought was occurring to her. When she spoke, though, her voice was still harsh.

"You really expect me to believe you weren't going to fuck her?"

"Of course not," Sandy snorted. "I wouldn't ... I mean, I wouldn't do *it* like that."

"What's *it*?"

"Have sex. It'd be my first time."

Silence roiled in the alleyway as Weiss and Eva were beset by the dissonance of a virginal Sandy, arrayed against his persistent but admittedly non-specific affect of romantic prowess.

The space between Eva's fingers was sticky with the huge man's blood, and from some frayed edge of her psyche, she felt an unhinged giggle rising in her throat.

"I mean I've done *stuff*. Lots of times," Sandy said, with a whiff of defensiveness. "But I've been waiting for, you know, someone special."

He paused then, and looked at Weiss curiously.

"Are you a virgin?"

"No, Sandy. I'm not."

Sandy processed this for several moments on the floor of the alley before his face split into a thrilled grin.

"Hot," he said.

Weiss rolled her eyes again.

"Where is everyone else?" she asked.

"They went off to some sushi place that Rochelle knew. I went to find you two because raw fish is too shiny, for me. Food shouldn't glisten. It's indecent."

Weiss locked eyes with Eva and gave a jerk of her head toward the street. Eva nodded, eager to flee the dangerous dark of the alley, and they both discarded their knives in a nearby trash heap.

Weiss hauled on Sandy's hands, muscles in her arms flexing and bunching as she lifted him to his feet. She draped his arm over her shoulder as they walked toward the street and Sandy leaned contentedly into her, pretending to need the support.

Eva fell into step behind them and found her hands were shaking, at last. She squeezed them into fists while casting glances backward as they worked their way out of the alley. Just before they reached the bustle of the street, she watched Weiss's arm falling down behind Sandy's back, her fingers dipping expertly into the back pocket of his pants. Weiss gave him a push as she did this, and in the brief commotion as they both staggered, Eva glimpsed the flat square of Sandy's personal plucked from his back pocket. A moment later, Weiss pitched the device into a passing trash heap, where it landed with a soft, nearly imperceptible thud.

Eva grinned, her teeth chattering with cold adrenaline.

"**CAN I** come in?"

Iskander paused, one boot still in the public car and the other settling with a crunch onto the icy curb.

"Come in?" he asked.

"Yeah. I want to see your place," Showe replied.

"I thought you had dinner plans?" As he spoke, Iskander folded his fingers into the hand sign for eating, adding the hooked finger that signaled a question. He knew by now that Showe could lip-read, but also that lip-reading was an imperfect art at best. He was working to improve his sign language, watching videos and studying guides at night.

Showe made a dismissive face. "That can wait," she said.

Iskander was still hovering, halfway out of the car, and he felt a fluttering, warm uncertainty in his stomach as she watched him.

"There's not much to see," he said at last, cupping his hand into a circle for "zero" and tapping two fingers near his eye for "see."

"I still want to."

"I'm getting ready to move – maybe you can come back in a few weeks, see my next place?" The sentence was far beyond his sign language competency, but Showe studied his lips as he spoke and replied easily.

"Is this like in crime serials where you murdered someone in your kitchen but are acting normal, and you planned to clean up the evidence, but some nosy hag from work is snooping and there's a close-up of sweat on your forehead?"

Iskander smiled somewhat dutifully, and Showe laughed.

"I just like seeing where people live! And I've seen sloppy bachelor pads before, if that's all you're worried about. But it's your place – if you want to keep it private, I respect that."

Her face was friendly and serious, and Iskander felt himself relax.

"All right," he said. "You can come see. But keep your expectations low."

The hand sign for "low" was a simple gesture that ended with lowering a hand from shoulder to chest, but Iskander exaggerated the movement, until he was bent over and his hand hovered as low as possible above the sidewalk.

Showe laughed and clambered from the car, and moments later they were sloughing through the snow. The car whisked itself down the street, ice crunching under its wheels.

"So ..." Showe paused as she took in their surroundings – drab cement blocks pocked with slitted windows, rising dourly from streaky snow. "These are apartments?"

"Yep."

It was mostly true. They passed a small sign, wooden and low to the ground, which read `Picochee County Supported Housing – Men's Campus`. Iskander quickly stepped forward to put his body between her and the sign.

"They're ugly, but it's not as bad as it looks."

His face swung away from Showe's as he looked around at the buildings with guarded fondness.

"I could have moved somewhere nicer a while ago, but ..."

Her tapping at his shoulder made him turn. Showe was regarding him patiently, and Iskander shook his head in apology, keeping his face toward her so she could read his lips.

"Sorry." He felt himself flush, but Showe made a practiced, dismissive gesture.

"It's okay," she said. "Why did you try to hide that sign back there?"

Iskander swallowed. Showe had pulled her personal from her coat and opened a dictation tool, where she could read his words as they appeared on the screen.

"It's just ... uncomfortable," he said at last. "Supported housing. They *are* apartments, but you have to get approval from the county to live here. And sometimes they force a roommate on you, whether you want it or not. I've been browsing rentals in nicer areas for a while now, but I guess these apartments have stuck to me a little more than I thought they would."

"They do look kind of sticky," Showe said dryly as she eyed the grubby cement walls, and Iskander covered a needle of hurt with a laugh.

"So, why haven't you moved out yet?"

He shrugged.

"I just know the people here, and the routine. If I move somewhere else, it'll just be a bunch of strangers."

"No family around here?"

"Nope."

"I get that," she said. "My knees were shaking when I went to sign for my first place, and that was with my mom and dad helping. I don't know how I would have managed by myself."

Her voice became hesitant.

"I'm sorry I joked about your home being sticky. Sometimes I talk before I think."

"It's okay." Iskander looked at her wryly, feeling something loosen in his chest. "It *is* kind of sticky, and that's why I *will* move out. Eventually."

More snow grated against their shoes as they plodded down the walkway, steps heavy and careful. Ahead of them, the sidewalk had a pale shimmer of ice, and Showe tucked a mittened hand under his arm, leaning against him as they stepped across. Even draped as they were in thick winter coats, Iskander keenly felt the pleasant pressure of her against his side.

They reached an innocuous door on the outer shell of one of the gray, cube-like buildings. Iskander waved his hand over the door handle and waited for the click before pushing inside, Showe following close behind.

"Whoa," she said.

"I can't keep a whole lot of creature comforts."

Iskander spoke matter-of-factly, with a skittering whiff of defensiveness.

"Stuff gets stolen a lot, especially if you work during the day like I do. One time they took my toilet paper, and it was halfway used up."

Iskander's apartment was a single, cold, aggressively undecorated room. His sun-bleached blue bicycle leaned against one corner, a chain as thick as a wrist securing it to the floor. A bed pushed against a wall, two spindly chairs, and a folding card table completed the sparse furnishing atop a carpet in the mud beige common to cheap living spaces across the universe.

Iskander flicked on a heater in the wall, which hummed with a surprisingly quiet and pleasant efficiency and wafted warm flows into the air.

Showe had looked up from the dictation on her personal and was surveying the room with a small, wondering smile.

"I get that, minimalist, but this aesthetic is tiptoeing toward serial killer. What's in here?"

She stood over a small cardboard box near the foot of his bed, its contents too dented and dog-eared to interest the room's periodic burglars.

"Just odds and ends I didn't want to throw out."

Showe was immediately interested.

"Can I look through it?"

Iskander shrugged and nodded, sitting down on the corner of his bed. He found he was intensely, comfortably aware of her presence in his room – a strange but welcome addition to the small, quiet space.

"Speaking of serial killers."

From the depths of the box, Showe had extracted a pair of thin blue gloves, disposable and bunched together with a rubber band. She held them by the corner and eyed him curiously.

"Don't worry, they're not dirty. Just a keepsake."

Showe turned them over. "These are medical gloves, right?"

Iskander nodded.

"I was a nurse, almost. Those are from Olde Mizule General Hospital, down on Croughton Street."

Showe regarded him levelly, her curiosity and confidence in her right to know more so apparent that it did not occur to her to state them.

"I couldn't graduate. I got good scores on the written portion of the exams but I always failed the practicals because of an allergy to those gloves. My skin starts to itch, and then it hurts. A lot. My fingers go completely stiff after about half an hour, so I could barely hand people tools, much less suture a wound closed."

Showe looked at him quizzically.

"So ... you'd never worn gloves before?"

"Sure, but not waterproof surgical gloves. When's the last time you wore a rubber glove for longer than a few minutes?"

Showe looked thoughtful for a few moments.

"I wear them all the time at the shop, to keep grease and oil off my hands. But fair enough, I guess most people don't."

"Right, and I sure hadn't. So, I didn't know until we started the practical sessions, like assisting during a mock surgery, where we were wearing the gloves for a long time. I could work through the pain, for a little, but eventually my fingers go stiff and I'm useless. I tried all the different brands of gloves, all different materials, powdered and non-powdered, allergy meds, ice baths, acupuncture. I got pretty desperate at the end with some homeopathic stuff, but none of it worked."

He shrugged.

"So, I had to drop out. But they don't start practical sessions until the last two semesters, so by that point, I couldn't get a refund on my A-credit."

"What's an A-credit?"

"Free school. Two years of vocational, or one year of high-sci or arts. They give it to you when you're raised in UU."

"What's UU?"

"Unaccompanied Upbringing."

Showe looked up quickly from the dictation on her personal, and for the first time, the look she gave him had caution in it.

"Oh. I'm sorry. I ask a lot of questions."

"It's okay. I wouldn't answer them if I didn't want to."

"I have one more – if these gloves are what cost you your career, why keep them? Why not a stethoscope or something?"

"They were free, and don't take up a lot of space." Iskander shrugged. "Well, I guess it just felt right, too. Like, they're not just a keepsake, they're kind of a reminder, too."

Showe regarded him curiously.

"A reminder about what?"

"About …" Iskander hesitated. "… trusting that things will work out."

Spots of color appeared on his cheeks.

"Sorry, that's heavy. I never really thought about why I kept them, until now, so I'm processing in real-time."

Showe grinned playfully as she scanned the readout on her dictation tool.

"Well, the first hour of therapy is free, but after that I charge 100 per hour."

He chuckled and she quickly broke eye contact, dipping back down into the box and bringing up a handful of printed photos.

"This is so old-fashioned!" Her eyes creased into delighted arcs as she fingered the thick paper and paged through the photos.

"People will steal personals, but nobody steals prints."

Showe nodded, somewhat hesitantly, before turning a photo toward him.

"She's in a lot of these."

"That's Rina."

Iskander said it without needing to look at the photo she proffered.

"That's a pretty name. Is she your girlfriend?"

Her eyes peeked above the edge of the photo to watch his lips.

"No," he said, making his hand into a fist and shaking it side to side.

Showe paged through the photos some more, then gave him a skeptical look.

"You absolutely sure about that?"

Iskander shrugged philosophically.

"What happened?"

"It's a boring story," he said, as mildly as he could.

Showe's face was ablaze with curiosity. "I love boring stories!" she cried.

Iskander blew out a breath. "This is verging on trauma dumping," he said warningly, but Showe only held up her personal so he could see the dictation tool was ready, its display enlarged to fill the entire screen, and he shook his head at her before speaking.

"I knew Rina since we were really little – her family volunteered at my group home, and we didn't really understand what it meant that I was in UU, and she wasn't. There was a boy in class who made fun of me because I tripped a lot – my shoes didn't fit and UU couldn't get me new ones – and Rina punched him in the crotch. That's about as much as it came up, until we got older."

Showe nodded for him to continue.

"Rina was kind of rich, and her friends all looked different from me – they had nice clothes and good hair, especially the guys, who were kind of circling around her at that point. I did just as well as them on tests, or in athletics and aptitudes. But it was like, here's this clique of bright, polished rich kids, and then me, with ratty clothes and a buzzcut, because cutting my own hair is free. It probably doesn't sound that bad, but ..."

Iskander hesitated.

"... anyway, for a long time she was right next to me. Like when one of her friends asked why I used lunch credits instead of paying with a personal like everyone else, she would squeeze my hand under the table and it felt okay. But after a while she just wasn't there, and I had to explain things like that by myself. So, I started sitting somewhere else at lunch, and things just sort of stopped."

With obvious difficulty, Showe endured several long seconds of silence from him before her face seemed to collapse with disappointment.

"*That's it?* Friends since you were babies and she's kissing you like *this*—"

Showe waved the photo in her hand – Iskander on his blue bicycle, the paint not nearly as faded back then, with one leg planted on the curb and Rina wrapping herself around him, unbalancing him as she kissed him deeply.

"—and you two stop sitting at the same lunch table and *that's it?*"

Iskander shrugged, again. Showe's eyes flicked back to the photo and her eyebrows crinkled unhappily.

"Were you sad?"

"I was," he said it simply.

"Was she?"

Iskander shrugged yet again, and Showe's laugh was incredulous.

"Come on, I know there's more! Nothing *actually* crazy happens in high school, except maybe a teacher is being a creep, or someone gets pregnant."

At the word "pregnant" Iskander tried to keep his face expressionless, but he could tell by the way Showe's eyes widened that he had failed.

"Oh." Her mouth hung open on the word for a moment. "I'm so sorry, you were politely telling me to fuck off, and I didn't get it. I'm really sorry. Fuck."

"It's okay." Iskander sighed. "It … stopped. We didn't even …"

He paused again, his mouth gone dry.

"… look, you're fine. It's just not something I talk about a lot," he said at last.

"But, then—"

Showe cut herself off, her face suddenly chastened, and Iskander realized the young woman standing in his room, holding pictures of his past life, had almost no capacity for duplicity. When she was curious, she asked, when she disagreed, she said so, and when she was embarrassed, her face curled sadly, as it was doing now.

He knew he should feel bothered by her questions, but after spending his life bending around other people, managing their perceptions to scrounge for opportunity, talking with Showe felt like releasing a held breath.

"… then why did we break up?" he finally asked. She brightened at once and nodded.

"Well, it scared me, and it scared her, but after things cooled down, I realized we were scared for different reasons. I was scared because of practical things – mostly money, and time, and putting off school and jobs. But Rina just brushed those concerns off – she'd had a nanny and then an *au paire*, so the idea of not having money, or a baby impacting your career, just didn't click at all for her.

"So, I thought – well, not that I even *want* to have a kid, but since we're talking about it, if you're *not* freaked out by the money or the timing, then what is the problem, exactly? She never really answered, but if it wasn't about *when*, then it had to be about *who*. I wish we had a big fight, and I'd shouted or said something mean, because then it might explain why we never talked again. But there was nothing like that. Everything just stopped, and then one day her parents – not even Rina, her parents – reached out and asked me not to come around anymore."

"Oof." The sound was playful but Showe's face was sad. "I'm really sorry, Izzy."

"It's okay, it was for the best. I genuinely felt like a family friend, like I thought her parents were happy about us because they saw *me*, not just where I came from. And I know that's not fair. They're parents, they just wanted to protect their daughter, but that's what it was – protecting her, like I was dangerous. And I guess Rina … agreed."

He felt his mouth twist, and covered it by huffing out a sigh.

"I guess a pregnancy scare cuts right to the center – it was fine when her parents got to feel charitable, and Rina could feel authentic because she was slumming, fucking a UU kid, but when I got too close they shut me out. All of them."

Showe's eyebrows were crinkled as she read the dictation from her personal.

"Are you sure Rina wasn't just scared out of her mind?" she finally asked, and Iskander blinked.

"Not because of UU, or you specifically, but just because she was a pregnant teenager? I'm not trying to butt into your life story – what you just told me is brutal, and unfair, but pregnancy is a big fucking deal, and an *au paire* doesn't change that. I can't imagine anyone thinking you're *dangerous*, Izzy, but you were a teenager – you could have just *left*. Maybe you think you wouldn't do that, but nobody thinks they'd bail on a kid, so single moms are magically sprouting from the ground, I guess. Just because her parents would have helped her, it's still a fucking *baby*. Her entire life, until the day she dies, changed without her consent."

There was silence in the room for several moments until she spoke again.

"Look, I don't want to speak outside my lane, and I don't really know anything here except that I'm truly, truly sorry for how Rina and her parents made you feel, but also, maybe go easy on a teenager for choices she made on the scariest day of her life."

Iskander was silent for a long time before he spoke.

"In *War Trolls 5: Troll Massacre Squad*, Captain Rex Shaft says the scariest day of your life is the *only* day you can be truly judged."

Showe looked up from the dictation on her personal and grinned.

"Shut the fuck up, Izzy."

He grinned back, then paused for another several seconds while Showe watched him curiously.

"It's ancient history now – she moved off-planet a few years ago – but I guess that time period might be more … complicated … than I've been thinking. And that actually makes me feel better about it, so, I'll think on that. Ummm … thank you."

She dipped her head in acknowledgement, and when she replied, her voice had softened.

"I'm sorry if I got a little stiff before, when you first told me you were raised in UU," she said. "I was just surprised and … I guess that probably didn't feel great."

Iskander shrugged.

"It's okay. It's nothing new, UU has a reputation."

"Really, though. I'm genuinely sorry. I know what it's like to have people learn one fact about you and treat you differently."

Showe's personal buzzed loudly then, the noise cutting above the whirring of the heater. She narrowed her eyes at the screen and dismissed the alert with a swipe of her thumb.

"So, if you need someone punched in the crotch nowadays, let me know and I'll be there," she said.

Iskander laughed, and Showe smiled at him for a moment, then took a single, long stride across the room to plant herself in front of him. She stood within arm's reach, so that Iskander had to tilt his head far backward to look up at her from the bed.

"So, nursing school was a bust. Why lift driving?" she asked, still holding his gaze.

Her need to see his lips move made their conversations pleasantly intense – focused and face-to-face, at all times.

"No school needed to drive a lift, just savings. Like getting my bike, as a kid."

He jerked his chin at the bicycle in the corner.

"I worked odd jobs, saved up. After a bit, I could get the bike. Bike lets me get even more jobs – courier, food delivery. Make even more money. Save that money, I can buy a lift. Lift gets me even more jobs, more money. Save that money, too. And so on."

"What are you saving for now?"

"A better apartment. And I'd like to get my liquid-loader cert, so I can handle cans with liquid cargo. I'm bidding on some used C-class nips, too, to replace the ones I blew up. After that, not sure. A house, maybe. I've always wanted a screened porch."

Showe shook her head in smiling disbelief.

"A house with a screened porch, from a bike. Something that big from nothing. I think that's really impressive, Izzy."

"Building a racing engine, inside a shop you personally own, is impressive," Iskander said ruefully. "Saving money is boring."

She reached out to run her fingers over his scalp. The movement was not fast, but it was sudden, and Iskander jerked as her fingertips touched his hair. She paused, her grip gentle enough to be a question, and he leaned into her hand. His skin was warm under her touch and she pulled softly at his head, turning his face from side to side, watching the lines of his face move with interest.

"I think it's the sexy kind of boring," she said at last.

Iskander reached out to hook his hands behind her knees. He let them rest there, feeling the warmth of her legs under his palms, where only a slight tug would pull her down into bed on top of him.

Showe's personal buzzed again. Her brow was furrowed as she read, and she tapped out a response with one thumb. Iskander's smile slipped.

"I've got to go in a little." Her face smoothed as she returned her gaze to him, and her tone was warm but matter-of-fact.

"I want to watch a show with you for a little, though. In your bed. I don't want to hook up, though – just watch a show."

Iskander said nothing, only signed "I really want that" with his hands, and she smiled.

He sidled over, making room for her as she climbed onto the bed next to him. They pressed their backs to the wall and she leaned against him, the weight of her head pressing pleasantly on his shoulder.

He reached for his personal and used it to flick on a viewscreen embedded in his room's wall. Nearby, the heater continued to hum agreeably, blanketing the room in wafts of clean, warm air.

End of Episode 1

Keep going to read a sneak peek from the next episode, *Thread Cutter*, as Iskander prepares for his debut fight in a lift battle tournament.

Help me out?

Reviews are <u>huge</u> for new authors, and if you have a few minutes, your honest review would truly mean the world to me.

Aim your phone's camera at either image below to leave a review.

NOTE

Amazon is happy to accept reviews even if you did not purchase the product on Amazon.

Sneak Peek from Episode 2: *Thread Cutter*

"**IN THE** gray corner, weighing 44 tons on the hoof ..." the announcer's bellowing voice paused, then lowered conspiratorially, "He's a terror in the night. He's a monster made of steel. He's the last thing you'll see under the dark of the moon! It's ..."

There was another long, grinning delay while the crowd leaned forward. "... Slaughtermoon!"

The crowd howled as Slaughtermoon-1 rose from its haunches to stand erect, an angular-looking lift with a ruddy red streaks crisscrossing its dark frame. The engine on its back had a coat of shiny black paint – even the four exhaust pipes that rose in arrogant spires gleamed black like dusky organ pipes. The motor snarled, belts and fans spinning furiously as it fed power to the legs and lifted the cab to standing height, before subsiding to thump out a loping idle.

Two ore slingers were mounted on the upper corners of Slaughtermoon-1's cab – large, funnel-shaped hoppers up top fed heavy chunks of ore to cannon barrels lined with electromagnets that flung the rough-hewn projectiles with shocking speed. The lack of cargo manipulators below the ore slingers indicated that Slaughtermoon-1 was a purpose-built battle lift, not a re-purposed daily driver. The dark lift yawed its canopy over its haunches, legs fixed in place as the upper half twisted, tracing the muzzles of its ore slingers over the crowd as they laughed and feigned terror, safe behind a nearly-invisible screen of electricized netting that surrounded the stadium and undulated like a spiderweb in the breeze.

Iskander waited three stories below the stadium, in an underground facility once devoted to shipping freight but now given over to infrastructure for the lift fights. He stood shoulder-to-shoulder in a crowd of other competitors, all leaning toward a viewscreen that covered an entire wall. Media feeds were piped in from hundreds of camera drones that flitted and swirled through the arena, capturing the proceedings in glamorous detail.

"And in the black corner, weighing 68 tons on the hoof …"

Another pause from the announcer.

"Her name? A legend. Her lift? A colossus. Watch out, before you get *burned* by …"

The announcer grinned as drums rattled through the microphone.

"… Cinder!"

In the league's necessarily unofficial record-keeping, drivers used the name of their lift to conceal their true name and identity. To avoid confusion, the league's records added a "-1" to the name when referring to the machine, rather than the driver, and the fight's after-action report would note that Cinder-1 had stood impassively, steely limbs and chassis painted its signature blazing orange, making no pandering motions or even seeming to acknowledge its own introduction. This dismissive serenity did not stop the crowd from roaring much louder than they had for Slaughtermoon.

Cinder-1 was a massive lift, made even broader by deep stacks of ablative armor layered over every limb, joint, and panel. Like Slaughtermoon-1, two ore slingers poked cannon barrels out from the upper corners of its cab. Lower down, twin demolition lances hung from the hip joints – bone-white poles thick as a watermelon and long as a bus, rigid but not quite sturdy enough to keep from drooping at the ends. Clusters of scaled-down ore slingers at the tips of Cinder-1's arms completed the arsenal, replacing the magnetic cargo forks used for daily work at the Picochee mitt. Like the rest of Cinder-1, the steely bouquets of gun barrels were painted a furious orange, but here the vibrant citrus paintjob was pock-marked by dozens of ventilation holes in the cooling shrouds that wrapped each gun.

Cinder-1's engine loped at a heavy but restrained idle. Unlike Slaughtermoon-1, Cinder-1's powerplant had no flaring exhaust pipes or decorative covers – just a dark, dense mound of steel and rubber embedded in Cinder-1's back, shuddering in place as it idled. Smaller panels around the main display showed Iskander and the onlookers raw video feeds piped from the fighters' cabs, one of which showed Cinder stepping decisively on the throttle pedal, giving Cinder-1's powerplant a single spurt of fuel. A brief, shattering roar burst from the motor before it wound back down to the grimly methodical idle. All the while, Cinder-1's limbs, guns and chassis remain motionless and unflappable.

The crowd murmured with excitement.

"I swear, as long as I have a face, that woman will have a place to sit." A lift driver near Iskander was staring fixedly at the in-cab display of Cinder as he spoke.

Another driver grunted loudly in agreement.

"Gray corner, please show us you're ready," said the announcer.

Slaughtermoon-1's driver was a round-faced man, middle-aged, with a thick beard and small eyes. He rested one hand on the control stick at his knee and gave the camera a thumbs up and a grin.

"Black corner, please show us you're ready."

Cinder gave a short, curt nod. She sat straight, her face smooth and her eyes fixed forward watching Slaughtermoon-1. Like every lift that fought in the league's matches, the armored cover plate installed over her fragile windshield was inches thick, but cameras and sensors studded its surface and splashed an interior screen with a real-time display of Cinder-1's surroundings, providing the protection of the cover plate without sacrificing the view of the open windshield.

The arena was a flat expanse of sand with a dense scattering of gigantic boulders, each scarred with holes, chips, and scorch marks. The boulders were large enough to shelter the combatting lifts from each other's gunfire, though larger lifts like Cinder-1 needed to hunch and crouch. At their starting points, however, both Cinder-1 and Slaughtermoon-1 were surrounded by open sand and had clear views of one another – a straight and open line of fire that was bordered, but not interrupted, by the massive stone blockades.

"That's positive control confirmed by both fighters!" The announcer bellowed, and the crowd shouted approbation.

"The battle pit will flash red three times, then yellow three times, then one flash green. At the green light, fighters are weapons free. False starts with movement will result in a reset of the match and a two point penalty. False starts with damage will result in an immediate forfeit of the match. If you understand, please say yes."

"Yes." Slaughtermoon and Cinder's voices echoed from their respective screens.

A broad smile sounded in the announcer's voice.

"Fighters, you may turn off soft-step mode!"

Slaughtermoon-1's horn sounded, high and piercing, to signal it had disabled soft-step. A moment later, Cinder-1's shattering siren blared its own alarm over the sandy arena, larger in every way than Slaughtermoon's, ricocheting the noise from every wall. The crowd covered their ears and cheered.

"Fighters ready!"

On the in-cab camera feed, Cinder leaned on the throttle and her engine roared up to speed, a hurricane of noise bellowing from the exhaust pipes as her motor clawed at its redline limiter and readied avalanches of horsepower for her limbs and weapon motors.

The arena was bathed in a grim red glow.

On-off, on-off, on-off.

A brilliant, warming yellow suffused the ground.

On-off, on-off, on-off.

A single burst of verdant lime splashed the arena as the muzzles of both lifts' weapons exploded in concussive waves of gritty dust, and a deafening crack of noise rattled the stands.

End of sneak peek from *Thread Cutter*

For sale now!

Acknowledgements

I was somewhat outraged to find that authors are expected to write a lengthy acknowledgements section, having just exhausted themselves (and sometimes their readers) by finishing an entire novel. Unsurprisingly, my first draft of this acknowledgements section was about seven sentences, but it was gently explained to me that this was completely unacceptable because many readers would rightfully expect much more. Readers have, after all, just given me enormous amounts of their time and attention, and leaving them with a single, short, witty (I thought) paragraph would not just be unconventional, but verging on rude.

I then questioned whether the wry humor present in my original seven-sentence draft could compensate for the lack of body content, and was assured (somewhat less gently, at this point in the conversation) that it could not.

Without further ado, then, the person I would like to acknowledge and thank most deeply is you: the reader. I may not know you, but I appreciate you all the way to my bones. You chose to read my book, and you did not have to. For that, I will always be grateful, and while I acknowledge that "thanking the readers" is a common thing for an author to do, I would like to dwell on it for a moment because it is important me – really, truly important to me – to try to communicate the depth of my feelings on this topic.

I wrote this book and its sequels in 30-minute increments, every day after my 9-5 job. I had been struggling to find a consistent writing regimen for over a decade, and what finally worked (for me) was staying at work for an extra 30 minutes before I drove home, each and every day. With such a limited output, the writing and re-writing of the *Belly of Salt* series took years, and while it was occasionally enjoyable or satisfying, it was more often depressing, unrewarding, and more than anything else – an order of magnitude more than anything else – it was just work. Furthermore, as my manuscript slowly grew in length, the sheer mass of a book series began to weigh on me.

30 minutes a day seemed like a puny, hilariously insufficient amount of time to write, edit, and generally manage my 100,000+ word creation, but it was all I could spare. There were days where I spent all 30 minutes getting only a few sentences just right, just a few dozen words out of 100,000+.

Although *despair* is a melodramatic word, it felt wholly accurate at times – imagine diving into a project in your home, spending hours working and then finding yourself at midnight, exhausted, at the center of a hurricane of mess so impossibly huge that you feel like crying at the idea of putting it back together, all while remembering that you have work in the morning. It was that feeling, multiplied many times over.

Suffice to say, it was not a great time, but I muddled through it and now (thank fucking Christ) here we are at the end. It's done now. It's in readers' hands – your hands – and so, now armed with some understanding of the arrestingly enormous amount of emotional and mental energy that this novel took from me, I hope that you, the reader, better understand why I did not want to write an acknowledgements section any longer than seven sentences, and also, what I really mean when I say:

Thank you.
Truly, *thank you*.
Thank you for reading my book.
I hope you enjoyed it.

More Acknowledgements

I want to extend thanks to all the friends, family, and colleagues who helped me stay the course during the writing of this novel. In particular: Erin, my first and best advocate, who had the hardest job of all – telling me when it was bad.

Additionally, here are some heartfelt thanks in the most intimate format possible (a bulleted list):

- The many soldiers and contractors I have met over the course of my career, particularly in the Army SATCOM and Tactical Radio (TR) communities. Your work informed the foundations of Sargasso, Ruger, and the universe of *Belly of Salt* as a whole.

- Andrew, for keen insights on the military. RLTW.

- The shark.

- Alix.

- Owen.

- Max.

- All the publishing and marketing SMEs who gave their time and attention to make this book possible.

About the Author

T.S. Chalk's first paid writing gig was creating user manuals for space-borne military hardware. He spent several years writing for the US Navy and Army, content with a steady paycheck and even receiving a Department of Defense security clearance (disappointingly, he has yet to encounter a classified document that is even a little bit interesting). He has written fiction as a hobby from childhood to present day, and in his late twenties, he began work on the manuscript that would eventually become the 'Belly of Salt' series. More years passed and he transitioned into the glittering debauchery of corporate middle management, while also finishing work on 'Belly of Salt' and finally seeing it published for the first time in 2024.

Today, he lives in Virginia with his family and can make a pretty good chocolate creme pie – the secret is using crushed saltines for the crust.

Thank you for reading.

HERON HOUSE
- PRESS -

Made in the USA
Columbia, SC
04 July 2025